# CHILDREN OF THE SKIES

## BOOK ONE · 1 · DESTINY

Cover art by Nick Acosta
Illustrations by Nick Acosta

Special Thanks to my mom, Sandra Bettis, and my aunt, Phyllis Bettis, for all their support.

To learn more about the COTS universe and author J. Everett Bettis, visit:
http://childrenoftheskies.com/

# CHILDREN OF THE SKIES

BOOK ONE — 1 — DESTINY

## J. EVERETT BETTIS

# DEDICATION

I would like to dedicate this book to the angels in my life that I call family and friends. There were days were I definitely wanted to stop and not believe in myself but they would not let me. These angels would motivate and give me the encouragement I needed to finish my first trilogy.

When the days got hard and I felt as if I couldn't make it they became my strength.

When times got hard they lifted me up and let me know they were there for me.

When finances got hard they opened their hearts and pockets and fed me.

Without these angels none of this would be possible. There are no words I can give for the gratitude and love I have for them and how much I thank God for bringing them into my life. I have been enriched by their presence and company and now dedicate these three novels to them.

# PROLOGUE

In the vastness of space, something was coming. A translucent wave built deep within the cradle of nothingness, looking for its prey. It was a living energy, boundless in size and beautiful to behold. The galactic winds propelled this kaleidoscopic juggernaut through space. Undetected by its prey, the powerful tide swept past Pluto with unnatural speed. Before long, it reached the rings of Saturn, unimpressed. Its long journey through the infinite left it seeking and hungry.

The wave was coming.

The distant sounds of a thousand crackling thunderbolts shattered and echoed through space. A tidal wave of color illuminated the blackness of the universe, churning and devouring the darkness in its path. This monstrosity searched for its mark with unyielding desire. It yearned to fulfill its purpose and would not stop until it reached its target. The eagerness was building within the vast column soaring through the emptiness of space. The immense cosmic powers growing within the wave could sense that its target was close. Its empty jaws would soon open to consume it. Its digestive juices would assimilate its mark quickly.

Finally, it was close; so close, in fact, that the color spectrum seemed to almost giggle with wicked anticipation. Past Mars, it spied its destination for the first time since the beginning of its journey. Now, with Mars at its back, there was nothing in the way. The target was now before it, ready to be devoured. This little blue planet yearned for the freedom that only the wave could bring.

With the force of a windstorm and the stealth of a killer, it continued to make its way to the final resting place, where it could dissipate into a cloud of multicolored vapor.

*Life on Earth would never again be the same...*

# PART 1

## GENISIS

CHILDREN OF THE SKIES: DESTINY

# CHAPTER
## ONE

The darkness of the night had been chased away by the sunlight that crawled over the African landscape. Shadows lingered in the sprinkled prisms of light captured for just a moment. A subtle crack echoed as a fleeing predator paused momentarily in the pursuit of its prey. Born of the genesis of a brilliant ecosystem so fiercely balanced. Forty-five kilometers south of Olduvai Gorge was a monument to archaeology, to the study of humanity. Footprints solidified in volcanic ash bore the first markings of what would become the Laetoli Footprints.

Maximus Curton had long felt a connection to the disentangled history that just waited to be tethered once more, to become a part of the story that speaks of the human species. As he stood atop a ridge, hands raised over his eyes, the Sadiman volcano appeared in the distance. Powerfully built with brilliant ebony skin and soulful brown eyes, he was sedated in manner. A quiet intellect and desire to absorb all the knowledge the world had to offer were betrayed by smoldering aesthetics.

"Eric," called Maximus over his shoulder.

Silence answered, along with a gentle breeze.

He did not turn, but as he spoke again, the authority in his voice bled through. "Eric, Lily, we must get moving. You can perpetuate your passive-aggressive bond of sexual tension once we reach the base of the next ridge."

Eric emerged from below the ridge.

Though as powerfully built as Maximus, his arms and legs were carved from thick, pale muscle from time spent in the company of humid rooms and machines. His strength and size were born of athletics, a contrast of function and brute force. A tan shirt, unbuttoned except for a few across the waist, was sweat soaked. Dark glasses covered his eyes, and a beaten-up satchel was strung across his torso. Lifting a large bag with a grunt, he moved toward Maximus.

Where Eric already seemed sluggish and tired, Maximus barely perspired as he looked out across the Savannah with a critical eye. "This is the cost of experience, Mr. Mack. You could have remained quite comfortable in an air-conditioned condo, spending your time hanging out by the pool. I am sure there are a great many dull minds missing you. Come on now, bring your pretty little handbag and let's go," chided the larger man without a smile.

Eric Mack was a second-year graduate student in physiology, who had made the unfortunate decision – depending on your perspective – to take on an internship through an interdisciplinary program, and he was hired as part of a work relief project with Professor Curton. Exercise physiology students were encouraged to branch out and branching out he had. "Ha, ha, easy for you to say, Doc. You aren't lugging around this pack full of bricks. What exactly does this have to do with why we're here?" Eric questioned.

"They aren't bricks, Eric. And even if they were, you should be quite comfortable given how many are rattling around in that yogurt you call a brain," called a voice from behind the two men. Lily was attractive in a way that was both charming and uncomfortable. The vulnerability that radiated from her was palpable, yet strength glowed beneath the surface, threatening to be challenged. Lily's hair shimmered even in the dust-blown winds of the Savannah. Glistening skin accented her fragile beauty.

The professor ignored both of them. "We are doing a little extracurricular activity," was all the professor would say. "Besides, we are standing at the crossroads of creation, the culmination of science and history. The footprints discovered in the ash radically changed the narrative of anthropology, the understanding of human evolution. A little bit of respect is in order, children."

He started forward, leaving behind Eric and Lily. Taking a few steps down the ridge in a series of calculated movements, his feet were sure beneath him. The two students looked after him with long faces, as they considered the same path down. Even as they took a few tenuous steps, Maximus, a man with a checkered and mysterious past, placed his feet upon stable ground once more.

Looking back up, he smirked.

THERE ARE MOMENTS IN LIFE THAT ARE SEARED INTO MEMORY— remarkable and powerful—they come to define you. Elizabeth Duncan had always felt that despite her seemingly uneventful existence, something extraordinary was waiting just beyond the horizon. At 5 feet 3 inches tall, with long, straight black hair and a thin physique, she might have appeared ordinary. She attended standard schools, achieved average grades, and was raised by loving, albeit unremarkable, parents who worked as mid-level accountants.

Yet, Elizabeth harbored a secret passion that set her apart: fashion. Her mundane routine transformed when she met a semi-popular fashion designer, a friend's uncle, who was immediately impressed by her sketches. Hired on the spot, Elizabeth saw her dreams beginning to materialize. Her job in the fashion industry was exhilarating, and recently, her personal life had become equally thrilling. She was dating the company's most eligible bachelor, who had just proposed to her. Although she loved him, Elizabeth hesitated. Her father's betrayal, discovered during an innocent childhood ride when she spotted his car at a motel, had left deep scars. She wondered if her fiancé could end up like her father, risking their future happiness.

Despite her fears, Elizabeth chose to embrace the possibilities of love. Their life together flourished until one afternoon when, eager to share the news of her pregnancy, Elizabeth returned home early. The joyous moment shattered when she found her husband in their bed with another. Devastated, she left without a word and never looked back. The subsequent divorce was a mere formality compared to the emotional turmoil she endured.

The true turning point in Elizabeth's life came with the birth of her daughter, Madison. Nothing had prepared her for the profound love she felt for Madison. Despite the challenges of single motherhood, Madison thrived, growing into a bright, cheerful, and compassionate child. However, as Madison entered fifth grade, troubling symptoms began to surface—severe headaches and double vision, initially dismissed as minor ailments, took a sinister turn one day at school when Madison collapsed.

Rushed to the hospital, Madison underwent a series of tests, and an oncologist was soon delivering the grim diagnosis: pineoblastoma, a rare and aggressive brain cancer that spread to her pineal gland. Elizabeth, reeling from the news, met Dr. Michael Keenan, who explained the severity of Madison's condition and outlined an intensive treatment plan. Confronted with the possibility of losing her daughter, Elizabeth's fears resurfaced with intensity, echoing the abandonment she felt in her youth.

Standing eye to eye with Dr. Keenan, Elizabeth's voice trembled as she voiced the unimaginable, "Are you saying... my daughter could die?"

"There is always a possibility," he replied calmly.

Pacing the room, Elizabeth repeated, "No, no, no…" unable to accept another potential betrayal by fate.

Dr. Keenan, attempting to provide some comfort, advised, "Let's not get ahead of ourselves. We fight one day at a time."

As Elizabeth sat beside Madison's hospital bed, watching her sleep, she resolved to fight for her daughter's life with every ounce of her being. In that quiet hospital room, amid the beeping of machines and the soft breathing of her child, Elizabeth realized that every fear she had faced, every loss she had endured, had prepared her for this moment—to be the unyielding protector of her daughter's light.

MAXIMUS LED LILY BACK THROUGH THE BUSTLING DIG SITE, WEAVing through the clusters of scientists and Dogon villagers who worked side by side with a shared intensity. The air buzzed with a blend of voices, clinking tools, and the distant hum of machinery—a stark contrast to the quiet suburbs of Indiana where Lily had spent most of her life.

"Don't get me wrong, sir, I'm thrilled you chose me to come on this expedition, and it's an experience I will never forget," Lily said, her voice tinged with genuine awe.

"It's a bit different from the suburbs of Indiana, eh, Lily?" Maximus responded, his tone light, inviting a smile from her.

"Totally!" Lily exclaimed, then paused, her curiosity piqued. "But I have to ask…" She trailed off as Maximus stopped walking, turning to face her with a seriousness that marked his chiseled features.

Maximus's gaze was steady, insightful. "I brought Eric along for the same reason I brought you. You both have great potential—don't make that face, yes, even Eric. But both of you are having trouble seeing past the campus. There's a great big world out here waiting for young people like you to realize your potential."

"Like what the mind can see, the body can achieve kind of thing?" Lily ventured, trying to grasp the full measure of his words.

"Why not? Look around you." Maximus gestured expansively. "This was all just desert, but we're digging up a whole civilization built from the human imagination." His words hung between them, heavy with meaning.

Lily couldn't help but smile, deeply moved by the vision he painted. Yet, her eyes wandered, not just to the unearthed wonders, but to Maximus himself—to his muscles, and notably, to the large scar on his bicep and tattoo that peeked from under his sleeve.

"Is that what the army did for you? Expand your limitations?" she asked, immediately regretting her words as Maximus's expression hardened.

"I'm sorry, I shouldn't have mentioned that," she added quickly, her face flushing with embarrassment.

They resumed walking, Maximus's glare softening as he considered her genuine curiosity and perhaps her bravery in asking.

"The army did many wonderful things when I was there," he began, his voice reflective. "We built hospitals and saved lives. They gave me the path to my PhD. I forged friendships that could never be broken. All of that almost makes up for the bad days. Almost."

Lily regarded Maximus, dying to know more but understanding the boundaries of his comfort. Their conversation paused as they arrived at an unsealed chamber deep in the ground below the dig. Dogon villagers were on their hands and knees around the entrance, loudly praying and chanting.

"They seem terrified," Lily observed, her voice low.

"This cavern is an ancient church. This is very sacred ground for the Dogon," Maximus explained, nodding toward an ancient Dogon shaman standing on a nearby hill. His age was hard to discern, but his eyes sparkled with youthful exuberance as he nodded to Maximus to enter.

"Be careful of booby traps," Lily warned half-jokingly.

"Now because it's a church, I'm not expecting booby traps. However..." Maximus's tone turned serious. "If I'm not out in an hour, you and Eric are to go straight to the embassy and declare an international incident."

"Are you serious?" Lily asked, a hint of alarm in her voice.

"No, not at all. Give me an hour then ask the Dogon to begin a search for me and then contact the university," Maximus replied with a grin that turned serious again as he descended into the cavern.

Inside the cavern, Maximus was wide-eyed as he shone his flashlight around. The cavern was ancient and undisturbed but felt somehow new at the same time. Altars and artifacts from a world long ago lined the cave walls. His eyes settled on a great scorpion symbol on a central wall, but his attention was quickly drawn to a beautiful dagger resting on the bones of a hand in reverence on the main altar.

The dagger shone despite the dust and shadows of the cavern, its hilt made of animal bone while the blade curved almost like a wave. Maximus lifted the dagger from the bone, half-expecting a trap, but none came. He bowed in respect to the Scorpion symbol before heading out to reunite with Lily and Eric, who were packing up equipment outside.

"Legend says it was used by a great warrior to liberate an imprisoned population long before the birth of Christ," Maximus explained as he placed the dagger on the table before them. "The dagger became a symbol of freedom for those ancient peoples."

"But I thought you said the cavern was an ancient church?" Lily questioned, her brow furrowed in confusion.

"Freedom is something worshipped as much as any God in some parts of the world," Maximus responded, his voice carrying a note of reverence.

Eric, who had been quietly observing, finally spoke up. "Well, I'm sure the university will think it was worth the expense of sending us all here."

"Oh, that's all a write-off. But the Dean will be very pleased to show this off to all the boosters," Maximus replied, though his tone carried a hint of disappointment.

# CHAPTER

## TWO

The past months had wreaked havoc on their family of two. Grief and anger now clawed at Elizabeth's heart as she looked upon her daughter. Madison seemed so much smaller than her own height of 4'9"; a stark reminder of how much the disease had stolen from the bright future that had once laid ahead of her. Madison's once long, black hair was now a short crop, a consequence of relentless chemotherapy sessions. She lay nestled in a hospital bed, the sheets drawn up to her torso, her listless eyes barely registering the cartoon murmuring from the television. Her vibrant olive skin had faded, sapped of life by the merciless disease ravaging her from the inside.

Elizabeth's heart ached as she watched her daughter, the stillness between them punctuated only by the flickering images on the screen. No parent should have to endure the helplessness of watching their child suffer, struggling to understand why someone so young, with so many dreams and experiences yet to be savored, should face such a harrowing ordeal.

A gentle hand on Elizabeth's shoulder drew her back from the edge of despair. She turned to face Dr. Keenan, whose presence no longer comforted as it once had. His visage was etched with the day's fatigue and a sorrow that matched her own, a stark departure from the doting, whimsical grandfather figure who had once made her feel safe and hopeful.

Over the months, Elizabeth had come to see Dr. Keenan not just as her daughter's oncologist, but as a pillar of strength and resolve. Yet today, his usually comforting demeanor was overshadowed by a grave solemnity; his smile, though tender, seemed a strained echo of better days.

"How are my two favorite ladies doing this morning?" Dr. Keenan asked, attempting his usual cheerful greeting as he approached Madison's bedside.

Elizabeth masked her growing disappointment. It wasn't that Dr. Keenan wasn't doing everything possible—it was that, despite his best efforts, Madison continued to decline. "I think I am doing better..." Madison said weakly, sitting up with effort, a grimace fleeting across her face.

A fleeting smile crossed Elizabeth's lips, admiring her daughter's resilient spirit in the face of relentless adversity. Dr. Keenan, pulling a chair closer with a labored grunt, tried to maintain some lightness. "I see your mother continues to make a case for your room being zoned as an arboretum," he joked, touching his wrist to Madison's forehead to check her temperature.

"An arboretum would be full of trees, Dr. Keenan. My mom would never confuse that," Madison replied, a serious yet playful glint in her eyes.

Dr. Keenan chuckled softly, "Indeed she would not. My mistake."

"When can I go home, Dr. Keenan?" Madison asked directly, her voice steadier than Elizabeth expected.

"That's actually why I'm here this morning. I believe we can have you back in your castle by tomorrow afternoon, if that pleases the princess, of course," he said, his voice hopeful yet tinged with an unspoken sadness.

Madison's smile was weak but genuine. Yet, Elizabeth felt a chill run down her spine; she knew her daughter's condition hadn't miraculously improved overnight.

Dr. Keenan suggested they step outside for a moment to discuss the logistics of Madison's discharge—"Just the boring paperwork and forms," he assured.

Before following him, Elizabeth knelt by Madison's bed, taking her daughter's face gently in her hands. "I'll be right outside, Maddy. If you need anything, I'm right here," she whispered, her voice thick with emotion.

Madison's response was bright, though her spirit was visibly bruised by disease. "I know, mom. I'll be fine."

In the hallway, Elizabeth's fears were confirmed by Dr. Keenan's somber expression. "She isn't better, is she?" she asked, not ready to hear the answer.

"I'm afraid not," Dr. Keenan replied, his voice low.

"Why would you lie to her about going home?" Elizabeth's voice was a mix of anger and despair.

Dr. Keenan paused; his demeanor gentle. "The chemotherapy has proven ineffective. The disease is progressing faster than anticipated. I didn't lie; I'm sending you both home because there's nothing more we can do here. She can spend her final days in comfort, surrounded by love."

Elizabeth's world seemed to tilt; her grief palpable. "So, you're saying my best option is to take my daughter home to die?"

Dr. Keenan reached out, trying to offer some comfort, but Elizabeth recoiled slightly. "I wish there was more we could do. At this point, it's about quality of life," he explained softly.

Tears streaming down her cheeks, Elizabeth took a moment to gather herself, then looked back into the room where Madison lay. With newfound determination, she said, "Maddy has more strength and courage in her little finger than any of us. If she's fighting, I'm fighting."

Without waiting for a response, Elizabeth turned and walked back into Madison's room, her resolve hardened. Dr. Keenan watched her go, his expression one of deep sympathy mixed with admiration.

As they prepared to depart from the site, Lily noticed a flock of local birds circling above in an erratic pattern, their movements disjointed and distressed. She nudged Eric, who was meticulously packing up the last of their gear.

"Look at those birds. Doesn't that seem odd to you?" Lily asked, pointing towards the unsettled flock.

Eric squinted up at the sky, his forehead creasing in concern. "Yeah, that's not normal. Birds here are usually harmonious. Maybe the dig disturbed them?"

Maximus, overhearing the conversation as he approached with the storied dagger secured in a cloth wrap, also glanced up. "It's not just the birds. Look at the dogs." He gestured towards the edge of the excavation site where several local dogs lay listlessly, their usual vibrant energy sapped.

The trio exchanged uneasy looks, their thoughts momentarily veering from the euphoria of discovery to the implications of their activities on the local environment and wildlife.

"Something's unsettling them, and I don't think it's just our presence here," Maximus mused aloud, his gaze scanning the surrounding landscape.

Just then, Eric spotted the village Shaman standing silently on a distant hill, his figure almost blending into the dusk light, save for the occasional glint of his ritual attire catching the last rays of the sun.

"Max, isn't that the Shaman?" Eric pointed out, his voice tinged with a mix of awe and curiosity.

"Yes, it is," Maximus confirmed, squinting towards the hill. "Our work here is done, so continue packing up because we can head home now. First, I've got to pay respect to an old friend."

Maximus trudged up the hillside, each step weighed down by a deep contemplation, his silhouette set against the dusky hues that painted the sky. The landscape was bathed in twilight, wrapping the world in a blanket of serene colors that seemed to echo the calm before a storm.

As he approached the Shaman, the elder's expression was a complex tapestry of wisdom and childlike wonder, especially as his eyes landed on the ancient dagger Maximus held. The animals around them, usually vibrant with life, now bore a melancholy air, their behavior a stark deviation from the norm, adding an eerie stillness to the evening air.

"Shaman," Maximus began, his voice carrying a mix of respect and urgent curiosity. "We've noticed the animals... they're acting despondent, and the birds are particularly disturbed. Is this related to our presence here?"

The Shaman's eyes briefly met the horizon, a deep knowledge flickering within them before settling back on Maximus. "Not your presence," he replied slowly, his tone imbued with a gravity that seemed to stretch beyond the immediate surroundings. "But rather what you have unearthed."

Maximus's gaze dropped to the wrapped dagger in his hands, a symbol of freedom and ancient power. "It is a thing of beauty, is it not?" he remarked, the reverence in his voice mingling with an underlying question. "Makes me wonder why you and your people didn't retrieve it yourselves?"

"Why retrieve what we deliberately concealed?" the Shaman replied cryptically. His tone suggested layers of meaning, secrets entwined with the history of the artifact.

"And you're okay with me bringing it back to America?" Maximus inquired, seeking validation for his actions.

The shaman only offered Maximus a sly look. "The time has come." This is yours."

"From one doctor to another?" Maximus probed, seeking deeper meaning in the shaman's words.

"Something like that. Perhaps from one brother to another," the shaman replied, his words carrying a weight that touched Maximus deeply.

Touched, Maximus affirmed his intention to safeguard the artifact. "I'll ensure it is preserved and respected at the university," he declared, though his tone held a trace of reluctance, suggesting a personal struggle with parting from such a significant relic.

"I thank you for the hospitality of you and your people," Maximus expressed his gratitude, his respect for the shaman and his culture evident in his demeanor.

"I thank you for what you have done and what you soon will do," the shaman responded, placing a hand on Maximus's wrist, his touch conveying a sense of impending importance.

"Now, your healing can begin, old friend," the Shaman said, his voice imbuing each syllable with comfort and an air of mystery. "When you first arrived here, you were burdened by a past you couldn't reconcile."

Maximus's gaze dropped to the ground, the weight of his memories pressing heavily on him. In the presence of the Shaman, he always felt a regression, a return to the innocence and simplicity of youth—a stark contrast to the complexities of the life he had lived. The guilt of his past atrocities hung over him, a dark cloud that never quite dissipated. The Shaman, perceptive as ever, noticed the shift in Maximus's demeanor. His eyes, though aged, were keen and empathetic, reading the tumult of emotions playing across Maximus's face.

"I have witnessed your transformation," the Shaman continued, his eyes briefly flicking towards Lily and Eric, who were playfully bickering nearby. "From a soldier wrought with conflict to a teacher fostering growth and resilience. You must embrace the entirety of who you are—

the light and the shadow—to become the man destiny has shaped you to be."

These words, gentle yet profound, struck a chord in Maximus. The Shaman's acknowledgment of his journey—from the battlefields to the classrooms, from wielding weapons to imparting wisdom—served as a poignant reminder of the distance he had traveled, both physically and spiritually.

"You can no longer hide from the world, nor from yourself," the Shaman advised, his voice a soothing balm to Maximus's unsettled spirit. "Acceptance is not just the path to peace; it is the road to strength."

Maximus listened intently, a mix of curiosity and solemnity on his face. "A great change is coming," the shaman continued, his gaze shifting skyward as if to hint at a cosmic event of significant proportions.

Maximus looked down at the dagger, pondering the shaman's words. "Good," he uttered quietly, a sense of resolve firming in his voice as he bowed reverently to the shaman before walking away.

The shaman turned his gaze toward the heavens. "After all these millennia, the wave has finally arrived..." he murmured, a profound sense of anticipation coloring his tone.

# CHAPTER
## THREE

In the dead of night at the Keck Telescopic Observatory, under the sprawling canvas of stars and celestial wonders, the routine had settled into a predictable lull. Timothy, one of the night shift technicians, was indulging in a game of Angry Birds on his phone, his legs propped up on the control panel. The casual flicks of his finger launching virtual birds across the screen were a stark contrast to the meticulous tweaks and adjustments being made by his colleague, Robert.

Robert, the more serious of the two, was engrossed in calibrating the equipment, ensuring every measurement and reading was precise. His brow furrowed in concentration; he couldn't help but cast disapproving glances at Timothy. "You need to take this more seriously, Tim. We're not here to goof off. We're guardians of one of the most sophisticated astronomical instruments on Earth."

Timothy rolled his eyes without looking up from his game. "Relax, Rob. Who's going to see me playing? It's just you, me, and the vast universe out here. What do you think is going to happen?"

As if on cue, the tranquility of the moment was shattered by a cacophony of beeps and blinking lights from the console. Timothy, startled by the sudden alert, sprang to his feet so quickly that he knocked over his coffee cup, splashing its contents over the tiled floor.

Both men stared at the monitors as streams of data flooded the screens—readings unlike anything they had seen before. The instruments were picking up something massive, an anomaly that defied immediate explanation.

"What in the world is that?" Timothy muttered, wiping his hands on his jeans as he leaned closer to the screen.

Robert, equally baffled, toggled between screens, trying to make sense of the readings. "I have no idea, but it's big. Really big. And it's moving toward us."

Their eyes met, a silent acknowledgment of the gravity of the situation. Timothy's earlier nonchalance had evaporated as quickly as his spilled coffee. "I think it's time to call the boss," he said, his voice tense.

Robert nodded, his hand already reaching for the phone. As he dialed their supervisor's number, his mind raced with possibilities. What they were witnessing could be a new discovery, a celestial body or phenomenon unknown to humanity. The implications were enormous, not just for their careers but for science as a whole.

The phone line crackled to life. "This is Jenkins..."

IN THE OPULENT MASTER BEDROOM OF ZACCARIE LORENZ'S MANsion, luxury was not just an accent but the very essence of existence. The room, adorned with exquisite antiques and impossibly rare art, reflected a den of indulgence that seemed more fit for a deity than a man. At the center of this lavish sanctuary was a bed larger than king-size, draped in the most luxurious silk sheets and crowned with a dozen perfect pillows.

It was here, amidst this splendor, that Zaccarie Lorenz, a paragon of elite beauty and muscular grace with salt-and-pepper hair highlighting his late forties, reveled in the throes of passion with Monique Thatcher, a woman whose stunning appearance rivaled that of any magazine cover.

Their union was a wilderness of passion, their beautiful forms locked in an intense embrace. Zaccarie, with his chiseled laugh lines and commanding presence, and Monique, a breathtaking vision of allure, were both members of the societal upper echelon—people accustomed to taking what they wanted. But even in such private moments, the real world could not be kept entirely at bay. LaMeire Desare, Zaccarie's grey-haired, impeccably dressed butler and protector, entered the room with the discretion and efficiency that marked his many years of service.

LaMeire stood patiently, his expression unreadable as he waited for his employer to conclude his activities. Monique, panting from their exertions, complimented Zaccarie with a mixture of admiration and post-coital satisfaction. "You are a master, Zaccarie."

Zaccarie's reply was tinged with disdain for her absent husband. "Too bad your husband isn't. He's nothing but fat, grotesque garbage. How can you stand it?"

"It has its advantages," Monique replied, her voice a sultry murmur, revealing the pragmatic side of her liaison with Zaccarie.

"Which you will share with me. Like a good girl does," Zaccarie said, slipping a small thumb drive into her hand as a token of their transactional relationship.

Monique's response was flirtatious, yet tinged with expectation. "Will I get my reward?"

Zaccarie ran his thumb over her lips, a gesture she welcomed briefly before he yanked it away. "You have to earn rewards in my kingdom," he declared, his tone suggesting both promise and threat.

LaMeire, seizing a pause in the conversation, stepped forward. "The meeting, sir."

"That's your cue," Zaccarie directed Monique, his tone dismissive, signaling the end of their private engagement.

As Monique reluctantly slid from the silk sheets and began dressing, she tossed a parting shot, her voice carrying a blend of defiance and flirtation. "My husband isn't afraid of you, you know."

"Good. That means he'll never see me coming," Zaccarie retorted coldly, his focus shifting from personal pleasure to the realms of power and influence. He had business to attend to, a reality that allowed little room for the softer distractions of life.

LaMeire, ever the efficient aide, assisted Zaccarie into a suit that cost more than many cars, erasing any evidence of the recent indiscretions. The transformation from lover to leader was seamless, a testament to Zaccarie's ability to compartmentalize his life.

"Dialec is prepared?" Zaccarie inquired as he adjusted his cufflinks, the epitome of boardroom readiness.

"The sooth sayer is waiting," LaMeire informed him, his voice as measured and formal as his posture.

"She can wait a few minutes longer," Zaccarie decided, pausing to reflect on another matter. "What else?"

"The Japanese markets are struggling just as you predicted, sir," LaMeire reported, confirming the financial foresight that had fortified Zaccarie's empire.

"They haven't figured how to ride all the waves our new inflation has brought to the market," Zaccarie mused, his mind always strategizing several moves ahead.

As they moved from the private opulence of the bedroom to the grandeur of the mansion's hallway, they were met with exquisite relics born from other eras and a blend of old-world luxury. As he strided through, as if he owned the air, he breathed his mind unexpectedly wandered through the corridors of his past. It was an unwelcome journey, one that tore open doors he had thought long since sealed shut. But there, at the edges of his consciousness, the name "Laurel" began to echo, pulling him further into memories he'd fought to suppress.

He saw her as vividly as if it were yesterday. Laurel sat on the lush grass of the university courtyard, bathed in sunlight, exuding a presence akin to a Greek goddess, utterly unaware of the effect her beauty had. To Zaccarie, she was not just physically stunning; her beauty seemed to radiate from within as much as from without, a rarity that could captivate any who beheld her.

Mustering the courage his father had once instilled in him about mastering fear, Zaccarie approached her for the first time, his heart pounding with a mixture of dread and excitement. As he drew near, fate played its cruel hand; he tripped, sending his books sprawling across the grass. The embarrassment burned hot on his cheeks, but Laurel simply smiled—a warm, genuine smile—and helped him to his feet. In that moment, all his nervousness dissolved under the warmth of her grace. Zaccarie knew, without a shred of doubt, that he would marry her one day.

Laurel was the embodiment of compassion, a stark contrast to the cold opulence to which Zaccarie was accustomed. She taught him to embrace life's lighter moments, to find joy in the everyday. In return, he introduced her to a world of luxury previously beyond her imagination. They walked a path sprinkled with laughter and shared dreams, but the shadows of Zaccarie's lineage soon began to encroach on their idyllic world.

When the time came to introduce Laurel to his father, Aegeus Lorenz, the patriarch of the Lorenz family, the atmosphere chilled considerably. Aegeus, a man carved from the bedrock of pragmatism and power, sensed an unwelcome softening in his son—a vulnerability he viewed with disdain. Aegeus had poured his life into grooming Zaccarie for a role that demanded ruthlessness and strategic coldness, a role that Zaccarie increasingly found himself questioning.

The opposition wasn't just from Zaccarie's family. Laurel's own brother, protective and skeptical, repeatedly warned her against the union. "He is no good for you! His father is a crooked man who deals with unsavory people," he would argue fervently, despite Laurel's defense of Zaccarie's character, distinct from his lineage.

Back in his own household, Zaccarie was constantly bombarded with reminders of his duty and destiny. "Take it from someone who knows, love is a nonsensical, distracting emotion," Aegeus would chide whenever the topic of Laurel arose. To these admonishments, Zaccarie once dared to retort, "Is that how you felt about mother?" The question invariably left Aegeus momentarily speechless, trapped in a rare bout of introspection that he swiftly shook off.

Now, decades later, surrounded by the success and power he had inherited and expanded, Zaccarie found himself haunted by the what-ifs of a life path not taken. The laughter, the light in Laurel's eyes, the simple pleasures they had shared—these memories were now bitter reminders of the cost of power and the loneliness of leadership.

As the twilight embraced the land outside his mansion, a melancholy settled over Zaccarie. The decisions of his past weighed heavily upon him, each a chain link in the fortress of solitude he had constructed around his heart.

A subtle cough from LaMeire jerked Zaccarie back to reality. He found himself in a secluded library, its recesses cloaked in shadow and thick with an air of foreboding. Seated before him was a Mexican woman adorned in purple robes richly embroidered with gold symbols and intricate patterns. Her jet-black hair was coiled elegantly into a bun atop her head, and an array of pendants and chains adorned her neck, each one more intricate than the last. On the street, she might have passed for ordinary, yet here, an undeniable aura of authority and intimidation radiated from her very being. She lifted her gaze to meet Zaccarie's, her voice steady and commanding, "Shall we begin, Nombrado?"

Zaccarie Lorenz reclined in the shadow-drenched library of his mansion, the flickering candlelight casting an almost spectral glow across the rich tapestries and the black drapes that shrouded centuries-old tomes. The air was thick with the scent of ancient parchment and the heady aroma of the fire crackling in the hearth. LaMeire, ever the silent sentinel, stood at a respectful distance, observing the scene unfold with a practiced eye.

Dialec, her presence as enigmatic as the tarot cards she deftly shuffled, was a study in contrast to the opulence around her. Her eyes, dark and fathomless, were fixed on Zaccarie with an intensity that bordered on the supernatural. The air seemed to thrum with the power of the unseen, a testament to the Lorenz family's deep belief in the potency of ancient rituals and unseen forces.

She shuffled the deck with practiced ease, the cards making a soft whispering sound that seemed overly loud in the hushed room. With a flourish that seemed almost theatrical, she fanned the cards out with a snap. Three times she shuffled, and each time a card slipped from the deck as if compelled by an invisible hand.

The first to fall was the Nine of Pentacles. "Providence," Dialec announced, her voice echoing slightly in the vast room.

As she shuffled again, another card escaped her control—the Devil. "Enslavement," she pronounced with a grimace. Zaccarie, leaning forward, his interest piqued, queried, "Me or others?"

Without answering, Dialec continued her ritual. The next card revealed was the Tower. "Change," she said ominously.

"What kind?" Zaccarie pressed, his tone a mix of curiosity and apprehension.

"Your great plans are being confronted by a great storm," Dialec responded, her eyes not leaving the cards.

"I have protection from every angle," Zaccarie asserted confidently, his voice echoing around the high-ceilinged room.

"You don't," Dialec countered sharply, her gaze lifting to meet his. "You could be the storm the cards speak of," she added, a layer of complexity to her previous statement.

"There are forces at play more powerful than even you, Zaccarie," Dialec warned as she shuffled once more, her movements more deliberate. Eagle Eye, standing motionless yet attentive, listened intently, her presence almost ghostlike.

"A great chaos is coming," Dialec continued, "the likes of which the world has not seen in millennia."

"That is my plan. You are seeing my destiny in the cards," Zaccarie declared, his voice firm, yet there was a hint of questioning in his tone as if seeking confirmation of his chosen path.

"But what threats exist? Will anyone betray me?? What must I know?" he demanded, his need for foresight clear in his commanding tone.

Dialec paused, her next words carrying the weight of centuries. "You are a builder of worlds, Zaccarie Lorenz, but the world itself sits amongst a vast ocean with currents raging around it."

She then cast several small bones atop the cards, her movements precise. "Beware the Eagle that clutches the knife, Zaccarie Lorenz," she intoned, her warning cryptic yet chilling. Eagle Eye's eyebrow arched at the mention, a silent acknowledgment of the prophecy's potential implications.

"I am the builder of this world," Zaccarie proclaimed, his confidence unshaken by the oracle's foreboding. "Mark my words, Dialec. I am the chaos you see."

As Dialec collected the cards, one slipped, fluttering to the floor. Her attempt to mask her reaction failed as she flipped the card over to reveal the Scorpion. The symbol of inevitable transformation and danger stared back at them, a stark reminder of the perilous path Zaccarie was determined to tread.

IN THE COLD, BOUNDLESS EXPANSE OF SPACE, EARTH AND ITS moon lingered like celestial sentinels, suspended in the vastness that stretched infinitely in all directions. Their silent vigil, a routine splendor to the universe, was suddenly disturbed by an anomaly—an energy wave, spectral and elusive, coursing through the cosmos with the urgency of destiny itself.

This wave, uncharted and undefined by human understanding, darted across the void. It behaved unlike anything ever recorded; it flickered in and out of existence, a phantom pulse that defied the laws of physics. One moment it was a visible torrent of energy sweeping towards Earth, the next, it vanished, as if slipping through unseen cracks in the fabric of reality.

Back on Earth, the phenomenon went unnoticed by the masses who went about their daily lives, wrapped up in the immediacy of terrestrial concerns. But high above, aboard the International Space Observatory, a small team of astrophysicists and cosmologists watched with bated breath.

Dr. Lee Hartson, tapping rapidly at his console, broke the tense silence. "Did you see that? It's not just moving; it's... fluctuating," he remarked, his voice a blend of excitement and incredulity.

Beside her, Dr. Suki Kumar adjusted the sensors to their maximum sensitivity. "It's like it's phasing in and out of our dimension. Can an energy wave even do that?" Her tone was skeptical yet tinged with a thrill that only a true scientist could appreciate in the face of the unknown.

"Whatever it is, it's not just a wave; it's like it's alive," added Marcus Williamson, the mission's data analyst, his eyes never leaving the readouts that flickered across his screen. His words hung in the air, a half-serious suggestion that nevertheless sent a chill through the room.

Dr. Hartson paused, considering the implications. "If it's phasing, it could be interacting with dark matter or... something else we haven't even theorized yet. We need to document everything. This could change how we understand not just space, but reality itself."

As the wave approached, its behavior grew more erratic, its appearances more fleeting. Yet each manifestation left behind a trace that the Observatory's instruments scrambled to capture.

Back on Earth, within the secure confines of a dimly lit situation room, government officials and military strategists gathered, their voices low and urgent. They had been forewarned by the vigilant technicians at the Keck Telescopic Observatory, and now, faced with the looming unknown, the atmosphere was charged with tension. Around the polished table, maps and screens glowed, casting eerie shadows on their determined faces.

"Could this be a weapon?" one official voiced aloud, cutting through the murmur of hushed conjectures. The question, laden with a mix of fear and curiosity, hung heavily in the air, echoing the deep concerns that pervaded the room.

"No," a seasoned general countered, his gaze firm. "It's more profound than that. We might be staring at a cosmic event that's beyond our current comprehension."

As debates raged and theories multiplied, the wave neared Earth, its intentions—or natural inclinations—unknown. Would it pass harmlessly or herald something transformative for humanity? Only time would tell, but for now, the world watched, waited, and wondered, united by a common sky and a shared mystery.

# CHAPTER
## FOUR

For as long as he could remember, Ron had been drawn to the pier at sunset. Despite the chill that often accompanied the ocean at night, he found a profound solace in watching day yield to darkness. Most people couldn't understand his fascination, often jesting, "How can you stand the ocean at night? It's freezing." But for Ron, it was more than just the daily twilight; it was a dance of the tides—raging, expressive, and tirelessly choreographed by the moon's gravitational pull. To him, it symbolized a persistent whisper of companionship in his solitude, softly reassuring him that no day was too hard to pass and that every sunset promised a fresh start.

Ron's attachment to the pier traced back to his childhood when his first foster mother would bring him there. With the backdrop of the vast sea, she would spin captivating tales about the stars and the deep waters, instilling in him a belief that dreams could indeed come true with faith and perseverance. Now, standing there as an adult, those once vivid dreams felt as distant as the horizon before him.

Life for Ron had unraveled into a series of disappointments—from a string of dysfunctional foster homes to fleeting friendships and unrealized ambitions. He had poured his heart into writing book after book, yet the elusive world of publishing continued to slip through his fingers like the fine sands of the beach below. His days were now consumed by the monotonous routine of an accounting job that, while paying the bills, did little to fulfill his yearning for a life of greater meaning and impact.

Determined not to succumb to a conventional life of silent resignation—marrying, having children, and settling into the predictable cadence of office life—Ron clung to a belief that the scales of fate must eventually tip in favor of those who had weathered great storms. Despite the relentless barrage of life's challenges, he was resolute in his conviction to seize a destiny beyond the mundane.

As he gazed up at the stars, memories of his foster mother anchored him, steadying his resolve against the currents of doubt that occasionally threatened to pull him under. Her stories at the pier had been his lifeline, a beacon that continued to guide him through the darkest nights. They reminded him that though the world had often been a harsh and unforgiving place, there remained a beauty in the promise of a new day.

Ron's reflections were momentarily interrupted by the sound of gentle footsteps approaching. He turned to see a woman standing beside him, her presence ethereal in the twilight. It was her—the foster mother from his childhood, or at least her image as vivid and nurturing as ever. "Beautiful, isn't it?" she remarked, her voice a soft echo of his thoughts.

"Yes, it's more than just a view; it's a reminder," Ron replied, his voice tinged with a mix of nostalgia and hope.

She nodded understandingly. "A reminder that no matter how the day ends, the sun will rise again, offering us a new beginning," she said, articulating Ron's own sentiments.

Encouraged by this unexpected encounter, Ron felt a renewed sense of connection—not just to the world around him but to the mysterious, familiar figure at his side. As the night deepened, they shared stories and reflections, finding solace in their shared experience by the pier, under the watchful guidance of the stars.

In that moment, Ron realized that while his journey had been fraught with trials, the path to fulfillment might just lie in these simple, shared human connections—affirmations of hope and the endless possibilities that each new day held. Then, as subtly as she had appeared, she was gone, leaving Ron alone with the stars and the gentle sound of the waves. Her visit, whether a figment of his longing or a spectral visitation, had reminded him powerfully of the beauty of life and the assurance that he was truly never alone.

Just as he was deep in thought, a dog—medium-sized, with a scruffy coat—trotted up to him. It looked familiar, like a stray he'd seen around the neighborhood, but something about its demeanor was different tonight. It barked at Ron, not menacingly, but with a sense of urgency that made Ron pause. The dog's eyes held a certain intensity, as if it were trying to communicate something important.

Ron bent down, extending a hand in a quiet gesture of friendship. "Hey there, what's up with you tonight?" he asked softly, trying to decipher the dog's distress. Instead of calming down, the dog continued to bark, each sound sharp and insistent.

Before Ron could react further, a voice called out from the darkness. "Rein! I'm so sorry!" A woman, likely in her thirties, rushed over, her expression one of mild embarrassment mixed with concern. She grabbed the dog's collar and pulled him gently away from Ron. "He usually doesn't act like this. I hope he didn't bother you."

Ron, who had stood up, offered a reassuring smile. "No problem at all," he replied, his tone light despite the odd flutter of unease that had settled in his chest. "He seems like he's trying to tell me something important."

The woman nodded, her brow furrowed as she glanced down at Max. "Yeah, he's been acting strange all day. Again, I'm sorry if he startled you." With a final apologetic smile, she led the dog away, leaving Ron alone once more.

Ron watched them go, the dog's urgent barking fading into the night. Something about the interaction left him feeling strangely unsettled. He turned back toward the ocean, gazing out at the waves that crashed and retreated in their endless cycle. The sea was a constant in his life, yet at moments like this, he felt more adrift than anchored.

He looked up at the sky, the stars barely visible through the coastal haze. The vastness above mirrored the ocean's depth, and Ron found himself wondering, not for the first time, where he truly belonged. The world seemed so immense, and yet he often felt invisible within it, his connection to places and people as fleeting as footprints washed away by the tide.

The encounter with the dog lingered in his mind, a symbol perhaps of his own restless searching. Was the universe trying to communicate something to him through these small, seemingly random events? Or was he simply trying to find meaning in the chaos of existence?

With a deep, almost imperceptible sigh, Ron turned his gaze back to the horizon. The sea whispered of distant shores and hidden depths, and he felt a kinship with its secrets. Here, amid the rhythmic lapping of the waves, Ron could believe that he was part of something larger, even if he couldn't quite grasp its contours.

Resolved not to let the night's serendipity go to waste, Ron decided to walk a bit further, letting the ocean's timeless song soothe his lingering unease. Perhaps, in the grand tapestry of the universe, there was a place for him after all, a thread that connected him to an unseen whole. And, just maybe, the answers he sought were waiting on the winds, carried by the waves that knew no bounds.

IN THE SHADOWY ALLEYS OF THE CITY, HOODED FIGURES DARTED with the kind of desperation that only comes when the blue and red lights of police cars slice through the darkness behind them. Sirens wailed, an urgent symphony that bounced off the wet concrete, as officers pursued on foot, their shouts almost lost in the cacophony.

"Stop!" An officer's command cut through the night air, sharp and commanding.

"In your dreams, copper! You gotta be faster than that!" one of the fleeing figures shouted back, his voice a cocktail of defiance and adrenaline.

Daniel, leading the pack, directed his crew with a sharp command, "This way!" His arm swung towards a rusted warehouse door that groaned on its hinges as they slipped through, disappearing from view just as the first officer rounded the corner.

Inside the abandoned warehouse, Daniel leaned heavily against a cold wall, his breath visible in the air. "Man, this is wilder than any video game, huh?" he gasped, trying to lighten the mood despite the seriousness of their escape.

Mason, always quick to critique, shot back, "You had to hit that last store, huh? Now we're out here running like we're in some bad action flick."

The distant clang of a door echoed through the empty space, snapping them back to the urgency of the moment. They bolted for the stairs, their steps a rapid drumbeat on the metal.

"Fortune's smiling on us tonight, boys," Craig called out as he spotted the ladder to the roof, his voice a mix of hope and relief.

They ascended quickly, slamming the hatch shut behind them. Mason, ever the pragmatist, barked, "Block that hatch!" Quickly, they scavenged the roof for anything to barricade the door.

Once secured, their escape continued with a leap across to an adjacent building, just as the sound of police reaching the hatch filled the air behind them.

Later, panting and finally safe, they reached the Iron Clan's hideout—an abandoned house that looked like it had been pulled straight from a ghost town. Inside, Jose Martinez, another leader of their ragtag group, awaited with a stern look.

"You guys sure know how to make an entrance," Jose remarked, his tone both amused and irritated as he surveyed the trio.

"Yeah, and nearly got snagged thanks to Tweedle-dee and Tweedle-dum over here," Mason quipped, nodding towards Daniel and Craig who sheepishly dropped their loot on the table.

Jose raised an eyebrow. "Trouble?"

"Nothing we couldn't dance around. Snagged two bags full of cash, though," Mason replied, trying to lighten the mood with a laugh and some fist bumps.

Jose cracked a smile as he peered into the bags. "Looks like Christmas came early this year, huh?" His comment drew chuckles and a few cheers from around the room.

He then clapped Mason on the shoulder, steering him towards the stairs. "Walk with me, got something important to show you."

They climbed to a private room on the second floor, where newspaper clippings and wanted posters wallpapered the space—a testament to their notoriety.

"I'm honored," Mason said softly, taking in the walls plastered with their past exploits.

Jose stopped in front of a family portrait that seemed oddly out of place in their gritty sanctuary. The younger faces in the photo, including a much younger Jose, looked back at them.

"These are my people. Some things... they're sacred, meant to be kept close," Jose explained, his voice thick with emotion.

Mason listened, a silent understanding passing between them as Jose shared his personal losses—the death of his parents, the crippling debts, and the painful spiral that led him and his siblings into foster care.

"Why tell me all this?" Mason's voice was barely above a whisper, a mix of curiosity and respect coloring his tone.

Jose's expression grew earnest, his gaze piercing Mason with a clarity that underscored the gravity of his next words. "Because you're not just a recruit; you're family now, Mason. And it's high time you understood the breadth of our ambitions."

Mason shifted uncomfortably, his emotions a whirlwind of confusion and anticipation. He faced Jose once more, his tone infused with newfound resolve. "And you've made this feel like a real family for me," he admitted, the weight of his past loneliness lingering in his voice.

Jose's nod was solemn, affirming their shared understanding. "We're far more than a mere gang, Mason. We're a tight-knit family. And now, it's time to elevate our game."

"Bigger?" Mason echoed, his curiosity piqued.

"Think about it, Mason. You believe I'm content with petty thefts and gas station hold-ups for forever? Not a chance," Jose said as he strode to a secluded corner of the room. With a dramatic flourish, he yanked down a dusty sheet, revealing a sophisticated setup: two desks cluttered with multiple computer screens and an array of high-tech equipment.

Mason's eyes widened in surprise as he stepped closer, drawn to the screens that flickered with lines of code and digital maps. Before he could formulate the question burning at the tip of his tongue, Jose anticipated his curiosity.

"Hacking," Jose declared with a hint of pride. "I've been dabbling in it since I was a kid. Turns out, I'm pretty darn skilled. We're evolving, Mason. The next chapter for the Iron Clan is all about cryptocurrency."

The revelation hit Mason like a thunderclap. The room, once just a symbol of their criminal activities, now felt like the nerve center of a burgeoning empire.

"I always pegged us as just a street gang," Mason confessed, his voice a mix of awe and confusion.

"We are a family, Mason. A family with a vision to break free from the constraints imposed by the big boss. He's been exploiting us for his own gains, but unknown to him, I have plans of my own," Jose explained, his tone fierce with determination.

Mason absorbed the information, the reality of their situation settling in. Here in this dimly lit room, their fates were being rewritten.

"This isn't just about survival anymore, is it?" Mason mused aloud, a spark of excitement kindling within him.

"No, it's not. It's about thriving. It's about taking control of our destiny, investing the fruits of our 'labors' into something that transcends the immediate. Daniel and Craig, may seem like two idiots, are smarter than they look. We've been funneling the proceeds from our heists into various cryptocurrencies, buying up properties left and right under the guise of a shell corporation," Jose elaborated, his fingers dancing across a keyboard as he brought up digital receipts and blockchain ledgers.

Mason stood there, his mind racing as he pieced together the magnitude of Jose's vision. What had once seemed like a makeshift family of misfits was on the brink of transforming into a formidable force with stakes in the virtual and real world.

"We're not just changing the game; we're rewriting the rules," Jose concluded, his eyes gleaming with a mix of cunning and excitement.

Mason, energized by the revelation, nodded in agreement, his own ambitions aligning with the daring path Jose had charted. As they stood together in the dim light of their makeshift command center, it was clear that the Iron Clan was no longer just a band of thieves—they were pioneers on the frontier of a digital revolution.

# CHAPTER
## FIVE

Zaccarie Lorenz strode through the resplendent halls of the recently restored Greek castle, his footsteps a soft, authoritative echo against the age-old stones. Situated above the serene Elounda seaside, this grand edifice was a symbol of power—a fitting backdrop for what was to come. The legacy of his family, deeply rooted in the occult and the arcane, lingered in every shadowed corner, a constant reminder of the destiny he was born to fulfill.

It had been days since his secret meeting with the enigmatic Bruja Dialec, a woman steeped in mystery and feared for her formidable powers. She had confirmed what he already knew: his fate was preordained, meticulously crafted by his father's relentless conditioning. Like a smith tempers steel, his father had methodically stripped away any flicker of compassion and self-doubt, forging him into more than just a man. Zaccarie had become an idea—an idea poised on the cusp of becoming a formidable reality.

As he walked, the echoes of his expensive black dress shoes rang out, a stark contrast to the soft crashing of the waves below. The castle, with its ancient stones and modern restorations, mirrored his own blend of ancient lineage and contemporary ambition.

Tonight was pivotal. He was on the brink of realizing a vision of divine governance, an era where a nation would revere him not just as a leader but as an emblem of power itself. Yet, amidst his ironclad resolve, an unusual sensation tugged at his consciousness—an uncharacteristic unease that he couldn't quite dismiss. This feeling, a blend of anticipation and foreboding, was alien to a man of his stature and experience.

Recognizing this stirring within as the weight of imminent greatness, Zaccarie reflected that many historic figures must have faced similar moments of introspection before their greatest triumphs. This realization didn't comfort him but instead heightened his awareness of the monumental changes on the horizon.

The shadows of the past, particularly memories of Laurel, flickered at the edges of his mind. Laurel, with her radiant innocence and stark contrast to his world, had once softened the harsh edges of his reality. She had taught him to find joy in life's simpler moments, offering a glimpse of a different path, one less burdened by legacy and power. Yet, those days were long behind him now, locked away in a chamber of his heart that he rarely dared to visit.

With every step towards the grand meeting room, where the future of his empire would be forged, Zaccarie steeled himself against the vestiges of doubt. Tonight, he would not just ascend; he would transcend, embracing fully the role he was crafted to inhabit.

As he approached the ornately carved doors of the meeting room, his resolve solidified. Whatever remnants of the man who walked the university's lush courtyards with Laurel were now just whispers of a bygone era, overshadowed by the titan he had become. Tonight, Zaccarie

Lorenz would not just step into his destiny; he would seize it with both hands and reshape the world in his image.

With a deep, steadying breath, Zaccarie opened the doors to the grand dining hall. Arrayed before him stood five men and one enigmatic woman. Nearest to him was the recently elected Prime Minister of France, Jean Francois.

"C'est un plaisir de vous voir de nouveau," Jean greeted warmly.

"Please accept my apologies for not calling sooner to offer my congratulations. I had a feeling the right thing would be done," Zaccarie replied, extending his arm for a congratulatory handshake.

"No apologies necessary, Zaccarie. There would be nothing to celebrate without you," the Prime Minister responded in fractured English, his tone conveying deep gratitude.

With a bemused grin and a raised eyebrow, Zaccarie acknowledged the compliment. "Yes, I am quite certain that is true."

Turning to his right, Zaccarie greeted another dignitary. "Secretary of State Allen, it has been too long."

"On behalf of the United States of America, I want to thank you for the generous gift," Allen said, his voice filled with official gratitude.

Zaccarie waved a dismissive hand, a blend of modesty and embarrassment coloring his gesture. "It was nothing; merely a show of good faith for my new friends."

"We won't forget it," Allen assured him.

"Thank you, my friend," Zaccarie replied, feeling the weight of the alliances he was forging.

He then bowed to President Zhou. "Ni hao," he said respectfully.

"Ni hao, Zorenz," the President returned the greeting, with a polite bow.

"For simplicity's sake, do you mind if we speak in English for the remainder of the evening?" Zaccarie suggested.

President Zhou agreed with a smile and a slight bow, appreciating the consideration.

Zaccarie's gaze then shifted to the last man, Premier Ludvig Ivonov, who looked back with a curious intensity. Known for his keen observation, Zaccarie understood that his ability to read people was part of why he was both feared and respected reasons why the most powerful figures in the world now gathered in this room.

"Premier Ivonov, thank you for coming on such short notice," Zaccarie acknowledged.

"When Zaccarie Lorenz requests your presence, you are sure to show your face," Ivonov responded, hinting at the influence Zaccarie wielded.

"You flatter me," Zaccarie said, a hint of sincerity in his voice.

Throughout these exchanges, the woman in the room remained silent, her presence an enigma. Dressed in dark, fitted attire and dark glasses that concealed her eyes, her sleek bun adding to her mysterious allure, she observed quietly. Zaccarie, aware of her silence, chose not to acknowledge her openly, yet her presence was palpable, her role a silent testament to the undercurrents of power at play. The others occasionally glanced her way, curiosity etched on their faces, pondering her identity and her role in this secluded, secret meeting.

Zaccarie gestured toward the ancient-looking grand dining table. "Gentlemen, please sit. Our dinner will be served shortly."

As they settled around the table, Zaccarie took his place at the head, feeling the gravity of the moment. "I thank you all for finding the time to meet as one family, to meet as The Vale."

# CHAPTER

## SIX

Elizabeth steered the car into the familiar driveway of their gated townhouse community, a place that hadn't been their home for long but had quickly captured her heart. The compact two-bedroom home was perfectly suited for her and Madison, manageable in size and demands, which was essential given Madison's ongoing health challenges.

As they approached the gate, Bernie Miles, the attendant, greeted them with his usual warm, welcoming smile. Elizabeth always felt a little lift in her spirits seeing him; Bernie wasn't just part of the reason she chose this community—he was its heart. His kindness and readiness to assist, especially with Madison's needs, were more than just helpful; they were a balm on her weary heart.

Bernie, with his silver-gray hair and Santa Claus belly that Madison teasingly remarked upon, was bustling out of his booth as they pulled up. "Well, there's my favorite girl," he beamed at Madison as he came up to the driver's side window.

Madison's face lit up, a sparkle flickering in her tired eyes. "Bernie! They let me come home today. Can you come over later and have dinner with me and Mommy?" her voice was hopeful, the invitation genuine and eager.

Elizabeth smiled at her daughter's excitement and then to Bernie, "You know you are always welcome."

Bernie's eyes twinkled as he nodded, "I appreciate that, ladies. When I finish up here, I'll be sure to come on over."

"Okay, Bernie," Madison's grin widened. "Don't forget."

As they moved toward the house, Bernie's question was gentle, reflective of his deep understanding of Madison's condition. "Madison, do you feel like walking into the house today?"

"I should be okay. I'm not dizzy today. Actually, I'm feeling pretty good, only a little tired," Madison responded, her voice stronger than it had been in the morning, filled with a quiet resilience.

"That's my brave girl. Okay, I'll see you tonight," Bernie waved them off, his gaze lingering with a soft concern as they drove away.

Madison continued to wave back until Bernie was out of sight, her spirits buoyed by the interaction. Elizabeth watched her daughter, feeling a mix of relief and sorrow that Madison found such joy in these small, everyday interactions—a stark reminder of the normalcy her illness often stole from her.

"So, what's one of the first things you want to do when we get inside?" Elizabeth asked, aiming to keep the buoyant mood going.

"I want to get into my closet," Madison declared, her voice firm.

"Your closet, why?" Elizabeth was curious.

"These clothes I have on smell like the hospital. I want to put on something that doesn't make me look like a ragdoll. You think we can go shopping soon?" Madison's question was hopeful, her thoughts already jumping ahead to more normal activities.

"My little fashionista," Elizabeth chuckled, her heart swelling with love and admiration for her daughter's indefatigable spirit. "If it's imperative, we can go shopping soon."

"After I take a shower and change my clothes, I want to play some Madden," Madison's plans continued, her energy seemingly boundless for the moment.

"Are you sure you're up for all that? You must be tired," Elizabeth's concern was evident in her tone, motherly instincts always on alert.

"Nah, I'm okay. I want to feel clean," Madison's reply was quick, her determination clear.

Elizabeth laughed softly, her heart lightened by her daughter's zest. "It still surprises me how much you love sports games. You're such a girly girl any other time. I swear, if I let you, you'd try out for the football team."

"I would, but they wouldn't be able to handle me," Madison joked, her laughter ringing clear and joyful as they approached the front of the house, their home—a sanctuary from the trials of the world outside, where they were, once again, just a happy family facing each day as it came.

Elizabeth descended the stairs to the kitchen, the familiar sounds of Madison's video game and her lively commentary to the television floated down the hallway. This comforting backdrop of noise washed over her, soothing her like a lullaby. It felt as though the harrowing nightmare they had endured was nothing more than a fleeting, misplaced dream—a moment of madness that had somehow righted itself, restoring peace to their home.

As she paced through the kitchen, arranging ingredients for the evening's meal. The savory scent of simmering spices wafted through the air as she set about chopping vegetables. Her movements were automatic, trained by countless evenings spent preparing meals in this very room, her sanctuary, now tinged with the shadow of uncertainty. The counters were cluttered, not just with the usual array of pots and pans, but with a scattering of overdue bills and final notices that seemed to multiply each day.

As she reached for a can of tomatoes, her fingers brushed against the stack of envelopes, each one a stark reminder of the debts piling up, threatening the fragile stability she had fought so hard to maintain for herself and her daughter, Madison. With a sigh, she pushed the thoughts aside and focused on the task at hand. The chili would be a simple meal, but comforting. Madison loved it, and tonight, more than ever, Elizabeth needed to feel that small sense of normalcy.

The pot of water on the stove began to boil, bubbles roiling up in a fierce, uncontrolled dance. Elizabeth glanced at it, her gaze then drifting to the window, the garden bathed in the soft glow of dusk. It was quiet, too quiet, and suddenly, the weight of her world pressed down upon her shoulders. The room felt smaller, the walls inching closer, suffocating. She leaned against the counter, tears welling up in her eyes as she considered the future. How many more nights would there be like this, making dinner in silence, each day blending into the next with no reprieve in sight?

In a moment of frustration, she swept the bills off the table, watching as they fluttered to the floor like leaves in the wind. The catharsis was brief. Gathering herself, she wiped her tears and bent to pick up the scattered papers, her movements brisk and a little too forceful.

It was then that the silence struck her—the absence of the usual background noise of Madison's video games coming from upstairs. Elizabeth straightened, listening intently. "Maddy, dinner is almost ready and Bernie will be here soon. Wrap it up," she called, her voice steady but tinged with concern.

No reply came.

Her heart skipped a beat. The kind of silence that filled the house now was unusual, unnatural. It pulsed with urgency. Dropping the papers, she hurried to the foot of the stairs and called again, louder this time. Still, no response.

Panic clawed at her chest as she raced up the stairs, two steps at a time. Reaching Madison's door, she found it slightly ajar. Pushing it open, the scene that greeted her sent a jolt of fear straight through her heart. Madison was on the floor, her small body crumpled, her hands clutching her head as she sobbed quietly.

"Mommy, my head..." Madison's voice was barely a whisper, each word a struggle as pain etched her features.

Without a second thought, Elizabeth scooped her daughter into her arms, her mind racing. Dr. Keenan's number flickered at the edge of her consciousness, but the immediate need to act overrode all else. She hurried down the stairs, her purse and keys already in mind.

She secured Madison in the back seat of the car, her hands trembling as she buckled her in. Glancing frantically towards the front gate, she saw no sign of Bernie, the security guard who was often a comforting presence around the neighborhood.

The car engine roared to life under her urgent hands, and she peeled away from the curb, tires screeching as she raced toward the gate. Bernie emerged from his booth, a figure of calm in the chaos.

"Bernie, I don't know what's wrong. She just started having a seizure," Elizabeth's voice was thick with panic, her eyes wide with terror.

"I'll call an ambulance right now," Bernie responded, his voice steady as he pulled out his phone.

Elizabeth turned back to Madison, her voice soft but desperate, "Madison, Mommy is right here. You are going to be alright. I swear it. I will not lose you." Her words were a lifeline, thrown in the hopes that they might somehow anchor her daughter back to safety.

As Bernie dialed for help, Elizabeth's vision blurred with tears, the world outside shrinking to nothing more than the immediate horror of the situation. The trees around them seemed indifferent to her plight, their leaves rustling quietly as if whispering secrets to the wind.

It was the moment she had dreaded, the moment that could tear her world apart.

Madison was dying.

AFTER RETURNING FROM HIS MOST RECENT RESEARCH TRIP, Maximus Curton found himself at the helm of his lecture hall, pacing energetically in front of a captive audience of fifty graduate students. The classroom, with its cutting-edge technology and sleek, futuristic design, might well have been lifted from the set of the Starship Enterprise. As he activated the interactive whiteboard, a detailed image of the human brain flickered into view, the lights dimming automatically to enhance the visual experience.

"The pineal gland," Maximus began, his voice resonating with the kind of authority that immediately drew all eyes to him, "is a midline structure located just dorsal to the superior colliculus; behind and beneath the stria medullaris, and between the laterally positioned thalamic bodies." He pointed with a red laser, emphasizing the gland's position, as the image zoomed in to focus on the reddish-gray, pine-cone-shaped gland.

"The gland is about five to eight millimeters in diameter," he continued, his clear, articulate speech echoing slightly in the spacious hall.

A hand shot up from the crowd. It was Lily, one of the students who had accompanied him on his recent expedition. Maximus had grown quite fond of Lily, whose petite stature and flirtatious demeanor masked a much more reserved and thoughtful inner life. Her high school years had been marked by tragedy and transformation, experiences that seemed to weigh on her during moments like these.

"Yes, Lily?" Maximus acknowledged her, giving a nod to invite her question.

"Isn't it true that, historically speaking, the pineal gland has been linked to metaphysics? I understand that metaphysics aren't grounded in empirical theory, but such early attention to the gland seems, well, connected," she asked, her voice a mix of curiosity and caution.

Behind her, Eric Mack let out a quip that broke the brief silence that followed her question. "Yeah, doesn't every good psychic have one?" His sarcasm, perfectly timed, sent a wave of laughter through the classroom.

Lily turned to give Eric a look that could have frozen lava, her expression one of amused exasperation.

"You're going to miss me when I graduate," Eric teased, undeterred by her glare.

"Ah, but you operate under the assumption that you will graduate," Maximus interjected, his tone light but pointed. "To do that, Mr. Mack, you'll first have to pass my class. And I assure you, I don't need my pineal gland to foresee the effort that might require."

Laughter erupted again, filling the room with a lively energy that reflected the rapport Maximus fostered with his students.

"Actually," Maximus continued, redirecting the focus back to the academic discussion, "Lily is correct. Many esteemed minds, both past and present, have attributed mystical properties to the pineal gland, often referring to it as the 'third eye.' This small endocrine gland in the vertebrate brain produces melatonin, which affects the modulation of wake/sleep patterns and seasonal functions." He pointed to the gland in the diagram. "Philosophers and theologians have even posited that the pineal gland could unlock the deeper mysteries of the brain and, consequently, its full potential."

As the clock struck three, the stir of students preparing to leave filled the air. "I know you're eager to leave, but next time, be prepared to discuss the nerve stems of the spinal cord," Maximus called out over the noise, his voice carrying a promise of more intriguing discussions to come.

The room began to empty, the bustle of students replaced by the softer sound of lingering conversations. "Mr. Mack, please wait a moment," Maximus called out as Eric began to follow Lily out the door.

Lily flashed Eric a supportive smile as she exited, leaving the two men in a suddenly quiet space.

"What did I do now?" Eric half-joked, half-groaned, turning to face his professor.

"I was hoping," Maximus began, his tone serious but compassionate, "that after spending time in the field this summer, you might start to appreciate what academic rigor can offer. We learn in the classroom to make informed decisions, preparing us for real-world challenges."

"I get that, Doc," Eric replied, his demeanor softening. "And I'm as serious as a heart attack. But school just doesn't feel like where I'm meant to be."

Maximus regarded him thoughtfully. "This life is yours to shape, not just a path laid out by others. But even the path you choose will require preparation. Consider that, Mr. Mack."

Eric nodded, a flicker of understanding in his eyes. "Can I go now?"

"Yes, you can go," Maximus said, watching as Eric took a moment before he walked out, perhaps pondering the weight of their exchange.

Maximus turned off the whiteboard and looked up into the nearly empty lecture hall, a sense of accomplishment mingling with concern for his students. He hoped that, like the mysterious pineal gland, they would unlock their potential, finding their paths illuminated by the knowledge shared here.

When the cosmic wave, charged with gritty anticipation, finally descended upon Earth, it unfolded as a spectacle beyond human comprehension. Rippling with otherworldly energy, the wave seemed sentient, rumbling with delight as it zeroed in on its distant, unsuspecting prey. The moon, a silent witness hanging in the vastness of space, seemed to tremble in terror, vibrating under the immense force of the wave as it thundered past.

This celestial phenomenon clutched the fragile blue planet in its ethereal winds—not with the grace of a dancer but with the relentless grip of a predator ensnaring its victim. In the breathless moments before impact, the menacing force transformed into a cosmic whirlwind of colors—a raw, untamed display of galactic beauty swirling across Earth's atmosphere.

Below, the world paused on the cusp of profound transformation. Cities, usually alive with the hum of nightlife, fell eerily silent under the alien lights that painted bizarre, long shadows across the awakening streets. People spilled from their homes, faces tilted skyward in awe and confusion, smartphones aloft to capture the spectacle, narrating breathlessly to their live audiences. The digital buzz on social networks swelled with wild speculations and exclamations, linking the global village in a shared moment of wonder and apprehension.

# CHAPTER
## SEVEN

### MAXIMUS CURTON

**M**aximus Curton's purposeful stride echoed in the dimly lit corridor of the Behavioral Sciences building, his mind already ticking ahead to the next class. Despite the exhaustion of a lengthy day, the lively debates about the pineal gland with his students had reignited a spark of nostalgia, reminding him of his own fervent freshman discussions about the brain's untapped powers.

As he turned a familiar corner, his office just a few steps away, the entire building shuddered slightly under his feet, and without warning, the lights flickered and died. A cloak of darkness enveloped the corridor, punctuated only by the distant, uncertain screams echoing through the building. In that heartbeat, the usual hum of the campus life was sucked away, replaced by a stifling stillness, broken sporadically by shouts and the sounds of scuffling feet.

The abrupt shift from light to dark left Maximus momentarily disoriented. As he paused, trying to make sense of the sudden blackout, a searing heat enveloped him. It wasn't just the absence of light—it was as if the very air around him vibrated with an unexplained energy, pulsating directly into his cerebrum with overwhelming intensity.

Confusion painted the faces of those around him; some students and faculty began to clutch their heads, staggering or dropping to the floor as if their legs had betrayed them. Others whispered in panic or cried out as they stood helpless in the face of turmoil.

Maximus, rooted in science yet open to the mysteries of the human mind, felt an alarming pain wrap around his skull. It clutched at him with a ferocity that demanded attention, pulling at the fringes of his consciousness with insistent fingers. As he staggered, trying to keep his balance, his surroundings spun into a whirlwind of shadows and screams. All his years of meticulous training and the disciplined resolve of an elite soldier were rendered powerless against the unyielding onslaught of this agony.

With a hand braced against the cool wall for support, he attempted to call out, to ask for help, but his voice was swallowed by the chaos around him. As the ground seemed to sway under his feet, his strength waned, and he crumpled to the floor in a heap, the cold tiles of the corridor pressing against his cheek.

The corridor around him, once a bastion of academia, now thrummed with the fear and confusion of a ship lost at sea. "Did you feel that?" a voice echoed in the turmoil, barely reaching Maximus as his vision blurred and dimmed.

"I think I'm going to be sick," another student moaned nearby, their voice tinged with the edge of panic.

In the grips of this mysterious force, Maximus fought against the tide of darkness that threatened to drag him down. His world reduced to a narrow tunnel of fading light, the echoes of the corridor distorting into an eerie symphony of fear and human distress. His senses dulled, and the reality of his environment slipped further away, pulling him towards an abyss he had only ever discussed in theories.

Then, a familiar voice pierced through the encroaching darkness, urgent and filled with concern. "Professor Curton, can you hear me?" It was one of his students, her face a blur above him, her hands possibly shaking him to keep him anchored to the waking world.

Maximus tried to respond, to muster a word or even a nod, but his body refused to obey. The darkness was a relentless foe, and as it wrapped its cold fingers around him, pulling him deeper into its embrace. As the last vestiges of light faded from his vision, the corridor, his students, and the surrounding chaos receded into the haze of a fading dream. He was adrift, succumbing to the void, and as his eyes fluttered shut, the fleeting image of a young girl's face hovered before him, a serene anchor in the tempest as he fell into darkness he saw the face of a young girl.

# ELIZABETH AND MADISON DUNCAN

AMIDST THE CACOPHONY OUTSIDE, DARKNESS HAD ENVELOPED the city, plunging it into an instant, unnerving blackout. The streets erupted into pandemonium as people, gripped by panic, scrambled aimlessly, their screams slicing through the air like sharp daggers. Something unimaginable had just occurred, shifting the very fabric of their reality.

The usual vibrancy of the city had morphed into a surreal tableau of chaos and confusion, illuminated only by the intermittent flash of car headlights and the distant glow of emergency services cutting through the haze.

By the time Elizabeth and her daughter reached the hospital, the scene was even more chaotic than the streets. The hospital was in overdrive, the air thick with the sharp tang of antiseptic and the low murmur of distress. Nurses and doctors darted through the corridors, their faces etched with urgency and concern, attending to the influx of patients that overwhelmed the emergency room. The wail of sirens and the clamor of medical equipment provided a stark backdrop to the unfolding crisis.

Elizabeth, struggling to maintain her balance, felt a sharp, stabbing pain in her head that seemed to echo the chaos around her. Her legs trembled, threatening to give out under the strain as she leaned heavily against a wall. The world around her spun slightly, the sounds and sights blending into a disorienting swirl.

"Mom, are you okay?" her daughter's voice broke through the haze, laced with worry.

Trying to muster a reassuring smile, Elizabeth responded with a strained whisper, "I just need a moment, sweetheart."

But her body had other plans. The pain intensified, a cruel reminder of her vulnerability. She slid down against the wall, her knees buckling as she succumbed to the overwhelming fatigue and pain.

Around her, the hospital staff navigated the surge of emergencies, their movements precise and practiced. Yet, in that moment, Elizabeth felt a profound isolation, as if the chaotic energy of the world was converging upon her, pressing down with an unbearable weight.

As a nurse observed her difficulty and came over, Elizabeth's eyesight blurred, darkening as she teetered on the verge of consciousness. Her final memory was of being gently placed onto a stretcher, the worried faces of medical personnel hanging over her, their voices a faraway echo. As darkness engulfed her, a tranquil calm swept over, bringing her to a short vision of a strong, reassuring man's face promising protection in the midst of the storm.

# ZACCARIE LORENZ

THE EVENING HAD BEEN SHAPING UP AS A COVERT SUMMIT OF power, with Zaccarie Lorenz presiding over a gathering that included some of the world's most influential figures. They convened in a grand room within an ancient Greek castle, now restored to its imposing splendor. The air was thick with the aroma of a rich dinner that lingered from their earlier meal, and an even richer undercurrent of clandestine discussions about the framework of their secret society, Cosa Nostra—a name chosen by Zaccarie, inspired by tales of power and secrecy his mother had whispered to him in his youth.

Years of meticulous strategy and maneuvering had led Zaccarie to this pinnacle moment. Surrounded by global leaders capable of tipping the world's balance, he relished in the irony that they were blind to the full spectrum of his ambitions. As discussions unfolded, Zaccarie's expression bore a clandestine smile, his mind adrift in visions of a future shaped entirely by his will.

However, the evening's calculated calm was shattered abruptly. Amid a debate initiated by Prime Minister Francois regarding Zaccarie's subtle tactics for dominance over the Five Houses, an abrupt screech of static from every electronic device sliced through the air. Lights flickered wildly above, casting eerie shadows that danced across the stone walls. The sudden chaos felt surreal, a collective hallucination shared amongst the most powerful.

Zaccarie, in a bid to steady the room, rose with authority only to be struck down by a wave of dizziness. His legs betrayed him as a sharp, tingling sensation surged up from his feet to his skull. He staggered, his situation deteriorating rapidly before the eyes of his esteemed guests. Words failed him, his voice a mere whisper lost in the commotion, "Is this an attack? But how—precautions were taken."

His fall was graceless, a stark contrast to his usual composure. As he hit the floor, the room fell eerily silent, the digital disturbance ceasing as abruptly as it had begun. Zaccarie lay prone on the cold, hard stone, his body seizing uncontrollably—a spectacle none had expected to witness.

It was then that the mysterious woman known only as Eagle Eye sprang into action. She deftly maneuvered through the shocked onlookers, her presence suddenly central as she administered first aid with a practiced ease. Her intervention was swift, placing a spoon in Zaccarie's mouth to prevent him from swallowing his tongue.

"What do you think you are doing?" Ludvig's voice boomed across the room, his demand for answers tinged with panic.

"We wouldn't want your precious leader to choke on his own tongue, now would we?" Eagle Eye retorted, her tone sharp yet composed as she managed the crisis.

"What is wrong with him?" the American delegate called out, his voice laced with alarm.

"Aside from the obvious seizure, I'm as in the dark as you are," she snapped back, her focus unyielding as she assessed Zaccarie's condition.

"We must get help," Zhou insisted, his voice shaking slightly.

"Don't be naive," the Prime Minister interjected. "Consider where we are. Our governments think we are elsewhere. We can't risk exposing this meeting."

Eagle Eye gave a curt nod, her expression grim but resolute. "I've got this under control," she declared, dismissing the men with a wave. "Please, leave."

The men, though reluctant, gathered their belongings and exited the grand room, each stealing a final glance at the fallen titan and the enigmatic woman now tending to him. The heavy doors thudded shut behind them, sealing the room in a weighted silence.

## JOSE AND MASON

AMID THE RELENTLESS BUZZ OF THE HOSPITAL EMERGENCY ROOM, Jose navigated through a sea of the afflicted, the frantic energy of the place enveloping him as he stumbled under the weight of his own pain. Patients lined the hallways, their faces etched with distress, while medical personnel moved with urgent purpose, addressing the burgeoning crisis that had overtaken the city since the cosmic event.

Jose urgently waved over Dr. Keenan, who was weaving through the chaos with practiced efficiency. "Doctor, it's getting worse," Jose called out, his voice tinged with desperation as he clutched his head, grimacing.

"Are you experiencing anything else besides the headaches?" Dr. Keenan inquired, his professional demeanor barely concealing his concern.

"My muscles, they're aching like they're being twisted," Jose replied, his voice strained. "Feels like something's writhing inside them. I've downed every painkiller I could find, but nothing touches it."

Dr. Keenan paused, offering Jose a swift visual assessment. "This sounds like more than just a simple migraine," he commented, his eyes darting across the overwhelmed emergency room. "We'll need to run some tests, but as you can see, we're swamped."

"I get that, Doc," Jose said, glancing down as he knelt beside another patient slumped against the wall—a young man sweating profusely and barely conscious. "Doc, this is Mason, my buddy. He's not waking up properly, keeps sweating buckets, and now he's got a nosebleed."

Dr. Keenan's brow furrowed as he quickly evaluated Mason. The emergency room had transformed into a triage zone, echoing with the cries of the afflicted and the urgent shouts of medical staff. It was clear that the bizarre symptoms were not isolated incidents.

The flashback to earlier in the day haunted Jose—a day meant for scouting their next move spiraled into an unforeseen medical nightmare. "Dude, are you okay?" he had asked Mason, only to receive murmured complaints of unbearable heat and exhaustion.

As they returned to their base, the sharp pains that had assaulted Jose's temples earlier grew into an unrelenting throb. It became apparent that whatever struck them was no minor bug.

Back in the present, Dr. Keenan's concern deepened. "Given the situation, we're prioritizing cases based on severity," he explained, his voice carrying over the din of the ER. "Mason needs immediate attention. We need to get him on a bed ASAP."

Jose nodded, the severity of Mason's condition overshadowing his own discomfort. "Sure, Doc, do whatever you need to. Just please, help him."

"Stay here. I'll arrange for assistance," Dr. Keenan promised, turning to address another urgent case. As he disappeared into the crowd, Jose remained at Mason's side, his presence a silent vow of solidarity.

The hospital's corridor, filled with the echoes of an unfolding crisis, resonated with a palpable tension. Jose stood firm by his friend, each passing second laden with uncertainty, as they waited for the medical intervention that could tilt the balance between recovery and despair.

# RON ETTS

DYLAN WEST HAD LONG SINCE OUTGROWN THE MONOTONOUS pulse of Kansas, where his childhood was stitched together with threads of adventure and solitude. With a look reminiscent of a young Brad Pitt, Dylan carried his charisma and caramel-brown eyes straight into the bustling heart of Los Angeles. As a reporter for KWTV Channel 4 News, he chased the adrenaline highs of police pursuits and political scandals. Yet, beneath the thrill of flashing cameras and breaking news lay an unquenched thirst for deeper exploits.

On this particular morning, as Dylan rolled out of bed and stumbled towards the kitchen, nothing hinted at the ordinary. Fetching his morning coffee was a reflex, but when he flung open the front door, a scene of disarray slapped him awake. His quiet neighborhood had transformed overnight: neighbors milled about in confusion, their faces lit by the eerie glow of headlights, and a strange hum vibrated through the air.

Before Dylan could process the chaos, his phone shrieked from the kitchen counter. It was Stacy Milburn, his formidable boss, her voice slicing through the haze of his confusion. "West, get your pants on and get in here," she demanded.

"What's up with the madness outside?" Dylan fired back, his mind already ticking through potential headlines.

"It's news, West. The kind you're paid to report on," Stacy retorted, her tone clipped with urgency.

"Copy that, on my way," Dylan replied, snapping his phone shut. Moments later, he was weaving through his apartment, grabbing his gear and dashing for his Mustang.

The drive to the station was surreal. Los Angeles's streets, usually a predictable stream of taillights and billboards, now mirrored scenes from dystopian blockbusters. Dylan dodged around accidents and navigated through the palpable panic flooding the streets. When he hit a snag near Ocean Boulevard, his reporter's instincts kicked into overdrive, but his thoughts were violently interrupted by a loud thud against his car.

Leaping out, Dylan confronted the source of the disruption—a young man with a bloodied face slamming his hand on the hood. "Hey, what—"

"Please... help me..." the man gasped, his face a mask of blood and desperation.

Acting on instinct, Dylan steadied the stranger, guiding him to the passenger seat. "What happened? Can you walk?" Dylan inquired, assessing the man's injuries with a mix of concern and professional curiosity.

The man, barely coherent, murmured about pain and pleaded for a hospital. Dylan nodded, quickly cleaning up the blood with a towel from his trunk and changing his shirt before slipping behind the wheel.

"Just hang on; we're heading to the hospital now," Dylan reassured him, catching the man's name—Ron Etts—between shallow breaths.

"I'm Dylan," he introduced himself, though his attention was split as his phone buzzed again—Stacy, demanding an update.

"I've got a piece of the story with me. We're on our way to the hospital," Dylan explained, his eyes flicking to Ron, who was now slumped against the door, pain etching deeper lines into his face.

As Dylan accelerated towards the hospital, his mind raced—not just with the urgency of Ron's condition, but with the realization that this day might pivot his career into new territories of storytelling. Beside him, Ron succumbed to the pain, his consciousness fading into a memory of a blond man with a discernible limp.

...WAVE

...within hours.
...describe a
...followed by a
...ocked people off
...widespread devas-
...s been dubbed the
...ts who are studying

...s suggest that over 2.5
...ve died as a direct
...e, with millions more
...Major cities
...hit with

Photo taken at Times Square moments after wave hit. New york City, car

...ddition to the immediate physical
...t has triggered

Repo
**Surg**

Sc

acc

tio

na

h

A Call for Unity and Resilie

As communities begin to rec

stories of resilience and solida

emerging. In cities across the

dents are helping one a

and fo

As the world around the
law of life concerns

ier today

Global Blackout: Mysterious Cosmic Event Leaves the World in Darkness and Disarray

## By Dylan West

In an unprecedented astronomical event, the Earth was struck by an unidentified cosmic energy wave late last night, plunging the entire planet into darkness for approximately three hours. The sudden blackout led to widespread panic and confusion, with numerous reports of people losing consciousness simultaneously across different continents. As of this morning, a significant number of these individuals remain unresponsive, prompting a healthcare crisis as hospitals struggle to accommodate the sudden influx of patients.

The blackout, which occurred without any prior warning, has thrown major cities around the world into chaos. Essential services were disrupted, causing traffic accidents and critical infrastructure failures. Emergency services were stretched to their limits as they responded to incidents ranging from minor accidents to large-scale emergencies.

Government officials have been quick to respond, with several countries declaring a state of emergency and instituting martial law in an attempt to maintain order. Curfews have been imposed in numerous cities, and military personnel have been deployed to patrol the streets and assist with emergency responses.

The cause of the cosmic event remains unclear. Scientists from major observatories and space agencies are scrambling to analyze the data to understand the source and nature of the mysterious energy wave. Initial reports suggest that the wave could be linked to a recently observed anomaly in the Van Allen radiation belts, but further analysis is required to confirm any theories.

"We are dealing with a phenomenon that goes beyond our current understanding of astrophysics," said Dr. Helen Choi, an astrophysicist at the National Space Research Institute. "The energy wave appears to have interacted with the Earth's electromagnetic field, but the full implications of this interaction are still unknown."

As cities around the world grapple with the aftermath of the blackout, the global economy has taken an immediate hit. Stock markets experienced sharp declines due to the uncertainty and disruption caused by the event. Governments are urging citizens to remain calm and stay indoors, promising that efforts are underway to stabilize the situation.

In the meantime, hospitals report being overwhelmed not only by those who lost consciousness during the event but also by individuals injured in accidents caused by the sudden loss of power. Medical experts are particularly concerned about the large number of unconscious individuals, many of whom show no signs of waking up despite having no visible injuries.

"This is an unprecedented medical challenge," said Dr. Emily Rivas, head of emergency services at a major hospital in New York City. "We are doing everything we can to care for these patients, but the situation is unlike anything we've ever seen."

As the world waits for answers, the resilience of global communities is being tested. The coming days will be crucial in determining the long-term impact of this cosmic event on the planet and its inhabitants. The international scientific community continues to work tirelessly, hoping to unravel the mystery behind the phenomenon that has already changed the world in unimaginable ways.

# CHAPTER
## EIGHT

*Three Days Later*

In the heart of a tumultuous Asian village, under a relentless midday sun, chaos reigned. The air was thick with dust and the acrid scent of smoke, remnants of a devastating conflict that had torn through the once-peaceful settlement. Villagers, faces etched with terror and confusion, scattered in every direction, desperate to escape the lingering danger.

At the epicenter of this pandemonium, Maximus Curton, a figure of commanding presence and unmistakable military training, moved with purpose. His muscular frame, built through years of rigorous discipline, maneuvered with agility uncommon for his size. His eyes, hardened by countless battles, surveyed the destruction around him. Clutching the hand of a young Asian girl, he guided her through the debris-strewn streets, his gaze never faltering from the path ahead.

"Change of plans, DeLorenzo," Maximus spoke into the radio, his voice calm yet urgent. "We need an exit, five minutes ago."

As they advanced, a figure emerged through the smoky haze—a woman soldier whose presence was as formidable as her reputation. Known only as Eagle Eye, her gaze was piercing and calculated, meeting Maximus's with a recognition born of many battles fought side by side. Her focus was unwavering, even as the environment around them threatened to spiral into further chaos.

Maximus, spotting a new danger, his voice boomed across the tumult. "Eagle Eye! Get down!!!" His command cut sharply through the noise of the village.

In response, Eagle Eye merely smirked, a flash of defiance in her eyes that spoke of her confidence and battle-hardened instincts. Then, as if on cue, the area around them erupted again—more explosions, closer this time, sending villagers diving for cover.

Maximus's sudden gasp shattered the silence of the hospital room, echoing off the stark white walls like a desperate cry for air. His body jolted upright on the hospital bed, a sound so fierce it could have been mistaken for a scream. Next to him, the attending nurse let out a genuine shriek, her shock mirroring the intensity of his unexpected awakening.

"Doctor, he's awake!" she exclaimed, her voice piercing through the calm of the medical facility as she dashed into the hallway.

Maximus, still catching his breath, ran a hand across his chest, feeling the steady rhythm of his heartbeat—a stark contrast to the chaos of his sudden revival. His eyes scanned the room with the sharp, methodical precision of a seasoned soldier, even as the phantom sounds of explosions, distant yelling, and harrowing screams infiltrated his senses. He could almost hear the terrifying cries for help, the agony in the voices calling out for loved ones.

The door burst open as the nurse returned, accompanied by Doctor Keenan, whose expression morphed from professional concern to outright amazement upon seeing Maximus conscious and alert.

"My God! Tell me, how are you feeling? What's the last thing you remember?" Dr. Keenan asked, approaching with a brisk urgency.

Maximus, instinctively, grabbed Keenan's wrist, halting his advance—a reflex from a past fraught with dangers. "What happened? Where are my students?" he demanded, his voice a mix of authority and concern.

"Your students are fine," Dr. Keenan reassured, gently extracting his wrist from Maximus's firm grip. "You've been asleep for a few days. Three to be precise. You were brought here after you collapsed on campus. Now, if you don't mind..."

"Please forgive me. Old habits from a former life," Maximus apologized, releasing the doctor's wrist.

Dr. Keenan, rubbing his wrist lightly, nodded in understanding. "Don't mention it. You have had quite a shock." The sounds of commotion from outside the room grew as more patients began to awaken.

"I'll come back and see you soon. But I must check on the others," Dr. Keenan said, turning to leave.

"Doctor, what happened?" Maximus called after him.

"Well, a few days ago, much of the world went to sleep, and now it appears you are waking up. Excuse me..." With that, Dr. Keenan exited, leaving Maximus to ponder his cryptic words.

Glancing at the clock, which read 3 PM, Maximus swung his legs off the bed and stood. The nurse moved to help him, but he waved her off with a quick, "No, I'm OK, I can do it." Despite the ordeal, his movements were surprisingly nimble as he walked to the bathroom.

Inside, Maximus caught his reflection in the mirror. Something was amiss. He lowered his hospital gown slightly, inspecting his arm where a scar should have been. His skin was unblemished, eerily smooth every battle scar had vanished.

Returning to his room, he found the nurse checking the medical equipment. "What's happened to my scars?" he asked, bewildered.

"I'm sorry?" the nurse responded, confused.

"I had...I had a number of scars. Where did they go?" Maximus pressed, his voice laced with incredulity.

"Sir, you had no scars when you arrived," the nurse replied, her own confusion apparent.

Maximus stood there, a mix of astonishment and suspicion settling over him. As he processed the nurse's words, the implications of his unmarked skin and the bizarre global slumber weighed heavily on him.

# CHAPTER
## NINE

Zaccarie, wrapped in dark silk sheets on an opulent bed, was a figure of profound concentration even in sleep. His unconscious mind navigated realms of memory and loss, painting vivid scenes of days both cherished and mourned. Amid the luxurious trappings of his bedroom, with the morning light streaming through grand windows, he seemed at once a titan of industry and a solitary man haunted by ghosts of his past.

As Zaccarie lay there, his sleep deepened by the lingering specters of his former love, Laurel, and his late mother, LaMeire Desare watched over him with a mix of professional concern and personal allegiance. The room, a sanctuary of wealth and history, was suddenly pierced by the crisp ring of a phone call.

LaMeire answered the call with a hushed tone, his voice barely disturbing the stillness of the chamber. "None. Not even the slightest flicker in his vitals," he reported, his eyes never straying far from the still form of Zaccarie.

On the other end, Eagle Eye's voice was equally low, laced with the urgency of their clandestine operations. "The hospital has no answers. Not yet, at least."

"You didn't say a word about him, did you? No one must know about his condition!" LaMeire pressed, his voice sharpening with the protective fervor that characterized his service to the Lorenz family.

"Calm yourself, LaMeire. There is no safer place for Zaccarie's secrets than with me," Eagle Eye responded, her tone as unwavering as the resolve that shaped her every action.

Their conversation was a dance of trust and necessity, played out over the lines of a secure connection. "Keep monitoring his condition. I'll be returning soon," Eagle Eye concluded before the line went dead.

LaMeire returned the phone to its cradle and resumed his vigilant watch over Zaccarie. The room was quiet again, save for the distant sounds of the estate stirring to life. But within moments, the peace was shattered. Zaccarie's body jerked awake with a gasp so loud it mirrored a cry of pain or fear, pulling him abruptly from the grip of his nightmares.

As his eyes snapped open, Zaccarie's gaze darted around the room, taking in the familiar yet suddenly alien surroundings of his own bedroom. His breaths came fast and shallow, the remnants of dream-induced terror still clinging to him. The dream of proposing to Laurel had felt so real, so close, only to be swept away by the crueler memories of her untimely death.

"What happened? Where am I? Where's Laurel?" Zaccarie's questions tumbled out, fueled by confusion and the raw edges of his dream.

"Easy Master Zaccarie. You gave everyone quite a scare," LaMeire said, stepping closer to the bed with a reassuring calm. His demeanor was a blend of the professional and the paternal, honed through years of service to the Lorenz lineage.

Zaccarie's mind fought through the fog of sleep and the sharper sting of reality. "The meeting with the Vale... tremendous pain... then darkness. Was I poisoned? I'll crush those—" he began, his voice rising with a mix of paranoia and command.

"No, Master Zaccarie. You were not poisoned," LaMeire interrupted, his hand raised in a calming gesture. "The Vale need you too much. Something else is at play here."

"You blacked out," he stated simply, his tone leaving no room for doubt.

"That much I've gathered. What I need to know is how I ended up here, in my bed, instead of where I last was," Zaccarie demanded, frustration coloring his tone as he tried to sit up, his body still weak from the ordeal.

"We had a global incident the moment you fell ill," LaMeire explained gently. "It wasn't just you; some are saying a third of the world's population experienced similar symptoms. You've been unconscious for three days."

Zaccarie processed this news, his mind racing with the implications. "Nothing will stop me. Not this incident, not even memories of ... her," he declared, his voice trailing off at Laurel's memory. However, as he paced the length of his room, his posture changed to one of defiance and pain, the resolution in his every stride matching the unwavering tenacity of his goal. His destiny.

# CHAPTER

## TEN

The tension in the secure conference room was palpable as key figures from the highest echelons of the U.S. government convened. The room, a stark, modern space within the Pentagon, buzzed with a mix of urgency and confusion. At the heart of the table sat Janice Albright, the enigmatic Director of National Intelligence, whose calm demeanor belied her secret identity as Eagle Eye.

Surrounding her were the nation's top officials, including the Director of Homeland Security, Alexandra Cortez, who seemed particularly on edge with a press conference looming. Dr. Anaya Persaud, the Science Advisor to the President from the Office of Science and Technology Policy, her West Indies heritage adding a layer of international flair to the discussions, shared her latest findings.

"The data from the Space Station and the observatory indicated unusual energy outputs right before impact," Dr. Persaud explained, her voice firm despite the murmurs of disbelief. "We had no precedent to predict the escalation into this global phenomenon."

The CIA Director, Frank Rutherford, a man known for his abrasive demeanor, interjected sharply. "And yet, with all our capabilities, we were blindsided. How did we not see this coming?"

Janice, ever the voice of reason, spoke up, her tone both soothing and commanding. "What we faced was beyond the scope of our known science. It wasn't just a burst of energy; it was a cosmic event that reshaped our understanding of the universe."

Across the table, the newly appointed Secretary of Health, Dr. William Hargrave—a distinguished white male with a background in public health crisis management—was sifting through reports. "We are compiling a comprehensive list of individuals hospitalized during the event. The patterns might give us more insight into the phenomenon's effects on biological systems."

Alexandra Cortez cleared her throat, bringing the room's focus back to the immediate concerns. "I have a press conference in an hour. I'll do what I can to buy us some time, but we need actionable information."

As the meeting adjourned, officials gathered their materials, the weight of the crisis drawing lines of concern across their faces. Janice approached Frank Rutherford, her gaze piercing. "Frank, what is AATIP doing about this? Any leads from their end?"

Frank scoffed, his response tinged with derision. "Advanced Aerospace Threat Identification Program? Janice, you know as well as I do—that program was dismantled years ago."

Janice fixed him with a knowing look, her eyes narrowing slightly. "Sure it was," she murmured cryptically, then turned to leave, her mind racing with plans and possibilities.

As she walked away, her thoughts were on the millions affected, the chaos unfolding across the globe, and the shadowy realms of government operations where sometimes, what was publicly known was just the surface of deeper, darker truths. The meeting had raised more questions than answers, but for Janice Albright, or rather, Eagle Eye, it was another puzzle to solve in her lifelong commitment to guarding national security from threats seen and unseen.

Ron had never imagined his cramped Los Angeles apartment could feel like a sanctuary, yet here he was, sprawled on his own bed instead of a hospital cot. The city noises, usually a cacophony that fueled his restlessness, today seemed subdued, almost respectful of his convalescence. He was alone, the doctor having decided there was no need for him to remain hospitalized after waking up like everyone else three days after the global anomaly.

With a groggy yet determined movement, Ron reached for the remote and flicked on the television. The screen lit up to reveal Dylan West, a familiar face from Channel 4 News, already deep into a report about the recent events that had shaken the world to its core.

"Good evening, Los Angeles," Dylan's voice filled the room, his tone a mixture of gravitas and intrigue. "In an unprecedented global event, millions fell unconscious simultaneously, only to wake up three days later with little to no memory of the incident."

Ron rubbed his temples, trying to piece together his own last moments of consciousness. He remembered the searing headache, the panic, then nothing until he found himself back in his own bed. As Dylan continued his report, snippets of Ron's own confusion began to align with the bizarre tales unfolding on the screen.

Suddenly, the screen split, showing a live feed from the White House where Secretary of Homeland Security Alexandra Cortez was about to speak. The urgency of the situation was palpable as Cortez addressed the nation.

"As of this hour, we can confirm that the phenomenon affecting millions globally did not result in any fatalities," Cortez announced, his demeanor composed yet visibly shaken. "Our top scientists are working around the clock to understand the source and implications of what we may well call a cosmic anomaly."

Ron's mind raced. A cosmic anomaly? The term echoed through his now-clearing fog of confusion. He recalled the strange, almost otherworldly sensation that had overtaken him right before he blacked out. Was it possible that what he had experienced was connected to this global event?

The broadcast returned to Dylan, who was now fielding questions from the public, his phone buzzing incessantly. "We've received countless reports of similar recoveries," Dylan relayed, his eyes scanning the incoming texts. "Families are being reunited, and individuals are reporting feeling healthier, stronger even, than before the incident."

It was as if a weight lifted from Ron's chest. He wasn't alone in this. Across the globe, people were not only waking up but also coming back changed. Was this the second chance he had always hoped for?

Just then, his phone rang. It was Dr. Elise Hammond, the neurologist who had been overseeing his case at the hospital. "Ron, it's Dr. Hammond. I'm checking in to see how you're doing at home."

"Better than ever, Dr. Hammond," Ron responded, his voice steady and more confident than it had been in days. "Do we know what happened yet?"

"That's still unclear," Dr. Hammond replied. "But the preliminary tests show that everyone affected seems to be experiencing a significant boost in physiological and cognitive functions. We're calling it the Reawakening."

The Reawakening. The words rang in Ron's ears, a fitting description for the inexplicable transformation he felt within himself. As he continued to watch the coverage, absorbing every piece of information, a deep sense of purpose began to take root. Whatever had happened, Ron knew he had been given a rare opportunity—a reset not just for himself, but potentially for the world.

And as he lay there, absorbing the gravity of his new reality, Ron felt a surge of determination. This wasn't just a recovery; it was a calling. Whatever lay ahead, he was ready to face it head-on, armed with a newfound strength and a mysterious but hopeful future that was just beginning to unfold.

# CHAPTER

## ELEVEN

Elizabeth stepped out of her car, greeted by a crisp morning breeze that caressed her face, offering a gentle reprieve from the usual hustle of the city. It felt surreal, this sense of vitality surging through her, as if the air itself was imbued with a newfound purity. For the first time in what felt like forever, Elizabeth felt an exhilarating sense of freedom, her steps buoyed as though she was walking on air. The persistent pains that had haunted her neck since Madison's illness had vanished, just like the nagging ache in her left arm that she'd endured since that fateful fall during a high school cheerleading stunt.

Her long black hair shimmered under the morning sun, its luster reflecting a vibrancy she hadn't seen in years, and her deep black eyes seemed to sparkle with renewed clarity. People often remarked on her porcelain-like skin, attributing its flawless appearance to her mixed Asian heritage—a stereotype she briskly corrected, though today, she couldn't help but marvel at its smooth, unblemished texture.

As she approached the hospital, the memory of that dreadful night when she thought she would lose Madison came flooding back. The streets had been ensnared in chaos, and the hospital had morphed into a war zone of despair. She remembered little from that night, aside from the overwhelming sense of helplessness that gripped her as Madison convulsed under the harsh fluorescent lights of the emergency room. But now, as she walked through the sliding doors of the hospital, the atmosphere was starkly different—a calm had settled over the place that had been absent just a week ago.

This change was miraculous, much like the cosmic event that had swept over the planet, rescuing Madison from the clutches of death in what many were calling a sign from the heavens. Others speculated darker origins, deeming it a harbinger of the apocalypse. Elizabeth didn't care for such theories; religious or not, the phenomenon had come at the precise moment to save her daughter, and for that, she was eternally grateful.

Now, a week later, she was back at the hospital to bring Madison home. The doctors had released Elizabeth a few days ago but had insisted on keeping Madison a bit longer for observation. As Elizabeth navigated through the quieter corridors of the hospital, she could hardly contain her excitement at the thought of bringing her daughter home.

Entering Madison's room, Elizabeth found her propped up in bed, a breakfast tray bearing scrambled eggs, sausage, and toast in front of her. The nurse was just adjusting the blinds, allowing the soft morning light to fill the room, enhancing the cheerful ambiance.

"Mommy!" Madison's voice, brimming with joy and surprise, cut through the calm.

"Hello, my sweet angel. How are you feeling today?" Elizabeth approached, her heart swelling at the sight of her daughter's bright demeanor.

"I feel pretty good," Madison responded earnestly, her youthful energy a stark contrast to the fragile girl of the past weeks.

"That's wonderful, baby," Elizabeth smiled, brushing a stray lock of hair from Madison's forehead.

"No, I mean, really good. The headaches are gone," Madison clarified, her eyes wide with sincerity.

"Of course, darling. Remember, you told me last week when you woke up that all that pain had vanished," Elizabeth reassured her, though Madison's next words caught her off guard.

"No, not just those," Madison pushed her breakfast tray aside, her actions full of youthful impatience. "I mean the really bad headaches I used to get before all this happened. They're gone too!"

Elizabeth paused, her hope mingling with disbelief. "Really? All gone?"

Madison's grin was infectious, her spirit seemingly unbound by any remnants of her past afflictions. "Yeah, it's like I'm totally back to normal."

Just then, Dr. Keenan entered, his presence a comforting constant in the tumult of the past days. "Good morning, Elizabeth, Madison. I've got some good news."

"Good news?" Elizabeth echoed, anticipation threading through her voice.

"It's time for Madison to go home. She's recovered remarkably well," Dr. Keenan announced, a smile playing on his lips.

Madison's excitement was palpable, her thoughts already leaping beyond the hospital walls to the freedom awaiting her. "Really? I can go outside and play?"

"Yes, you can," Dr. Keenan nodded, his eyes reflecting his professional satisfaction with her recovery.

Elizabeth's heart lifted. The nightmare was over. As they prepared to leave, she couldn't help but feel that the worst was behind them, and ahead lay only bright, hopeful days.

ELIZABETH LINKED HER ARM THROUGH DR. KEENAN'S AS THEY walked down the hallway, their steps light with the promise of new beginnings. The hospital, once a place of heartache and anxiety, now felt like a passageway back to the life they had temporarily lost.

"Madison has truly made a miraculous recovery," Dr. Keenan remarked, his voice imbued with a mix of professional awe and genuine relief. "It's rare to see such a rapid turnaround without any lingering complications."

Elizabeth smiled, her eyes brimming with unshed tears of joy. "It feels like we've been given a second chance. I can't thank you enough, Dr. Keenan."

As they approached the exit, the sunlight spilled through the glass doors, bathing the corridor in a warm, golden glow. Outside, the world seemed to have regained its rhythm, the normalcy of daily life resuming as if nothing had ever happened. Cars passed by, people chatted on their phones, and the faint sounds of laughter from a nearby park filled the air.

Madison skipped ahead, her energy boundless, her laughter a melody that Elizabeth had feared she might never hear again. "Come on, Mom! Let's go home!"

Catching up to her daughter, Elizabeth felt the weight of the past weeks lift from her shoulders. The fear and uncertainty that had gripped her heart were now replaced by an overwhelming sense of gratitude and hope.

As they reached their car, Madison turned to Dr. Keenan, her expression serious for a moment. "Dr. Keenan, you said a lot of people got sick like me, right? Did everyone get better?"

Dr. Keenan's smile faltered slightly, the reminder of the global scale of the incident sobering. "Many have recovered, Madison, but not everyone was as fortunate as you. The world is still trying to understand exactly what happened and why."

Madison nodded, her brow furrowed in thought. "We should do something to help them, Mommy."

Elizabeth exchanged a glance with Dr. Keenan, pride swelling in her chest. "We will, sweetheart. We'll think of something we can do as a family."

As they drove away from the hospital, the cityscape rolling past, Elizabeth's thoughts turned to the future. The phenomenon that had brought them to the brink of despair had also ushered in a new era of possibilities. With Madison's suggestion ringing in her ears, Elizabeth felt a renewed purpose. They had been given a second chance not just to live but to make a difference.

The drive home was quiet, contemplative. As they turned into their neighborhood, the familiar sights of their community welcomed them—a stark contrast to the chaos of just a week ago. Neighbors waved as they passed by, smiles wide and genuine.

Once home, Madison ran ahead, bursting through the front door with the eagerness of someone who had been away too long. Elizabeth followed at a slower pace, savoring the moment, the normalcy of coming home.

Inside, the house was just as they had left it, yet everything felt different—everything was more precious. As Madison raced around, rediscovering her toys and books, Elizabeth went to her room and sat by the window, looking out at the world that had changed so irrevocably.

The cosmic event might have receded into the background of global news, but its effects were indelibly imprinted on their lives. With Madison's recovery as a constant reminder of their fortune, Elizabeth knew their story was just one of many, each with its own shades of darkness and light.

Determined to contribute to the global healing process, Elizabeth began to outline plans for a community project, one that would help those still suffering from the aftermath of the mysterious cosmic phenomenon. Her thoughts were detailed and expansive, envisioning a campaign that could potentially reach millions.

As the sun set, casting long shadows across her notepad, Elizabeth felt a deep connection to the world beyond her window. The challenges were many, but for the first time in a long while, she felt equipped to face them, inspired by her daughter's resilience and the unexpected second chance they had both been granted.

# CHAPTER

## TWELVE

Maximus Curton stood at the edge of his expansive loft, gazing out through the floor-to-ceiling windows that framed the city's sprawling skyline. The converted warehouse offered an open expanse of space, the high ceilings and exposed brick walls a stark contrast to the claustrophobic confines he so deeply loathed. Small spaces reminded him too much of his past—a labyrinth of shadowy corridors and sealed rooms that held secrets he'd rather forget.

The loft was minimalist but warm, each piece of contemporary furniture chosen for both form and function. The vastness of the space usually brought him comfort, but tonight, the quiet pressed in around him like an invisible cage. The silence was palpable, broken only by the distant hum of traffic and the occasional siren wailing somewhere far below.

He sank into a leather armchair near the window, the city lights flickering like distant stars. Memories flooded his mind unbidden: the abrupt blackout, waking disoriented in a hospital bed, and most vividly, the woman from his vision. Her jet-black hair framed a face of serene beauty, her eyes dark pools that seemed to hold the mysteries of the universe. The way she smiled at him—a gentle curve of her lips that spoke of understanding and acceptance—had stirred something deep within him. When she placed her hand softly on his face, he felt an overwhelming sense of ease and contentment, a feeling of home he hadn't experienced in years.

The thought of her brought a bittersweet ache. It reminded him of those he'd lost, of connections severed by time and circumstance. The memory of his sister nudged at the corners of his mind, but he pushed it away as he always did. Thinking about her was like touching a raw nerve—too painful and laden with guilt. He had let her down, just as he had failed others who had depended on him.

Needing a distraction, Max rose and walked to the open-plan kitchen. He pulled a tumbler from the cabinet and reached for the bottle of bourbon that stood sentinel on the counter. Pouring a generous measure, he watched the amber liquid swirl, catching the soft glow of the pendant lights above. He took a slow sip, the warmth spreading through his chest, a temporary reprieve from the chill of isolation.

He was eager to return to work, to immerse himself in the structured world of academia where he could lose himself in research and lectures. But the bureaucratic machine at the university had other plans. Pressured by current events—the mysterious global blackout and its aftermath—they had asked him to take a short administrative leave. They insisted it was for his own good, but he knew better. It was easier for them to sideline him than to deal with the complications his presence might bring.

"So here I am," he muttered to himself, "drinking alone and thinking too much."

He set the glass down with a little more force than intended, the clink echoing in the emptiness. Restlessness gnawed at him. Sitting idle was never his forte. Max needed to be doing something, anything, to keep the shadows at bay.

His gaze drifted to a canvas propped against the far wall—an unfinished painting he'd abandoned months ago. Without overthinking it, he crossed the room, picking up a palette and brush. The act of mixing colors, the scent of oils and acrylics, had always been therapeutic. He began to paint, broad strokes that soon evolved into more intricate details.

As he worked, the image of the woman from his vision began to take shape on the canvas. Her eyes emerged first—deep and enigmatic—followed by the delicate lines of her face, the cascade of her dark hair. Time slipped away as he became absorbed in the process, the outside world fading into the background.

A soft chime broke his concentration. He glanced over to see his phone vibrating on the counter, the screen illuminating with a call from Christopher Cutty. Max considered ignoring it but thought better of it. Wiping his hands on a rag, he walked over and picked up.

"Evening, Chris," he answered, trying to keep his tone neutral.

"Max! Just checking in on you, buddy," Chris's voice chimed, overly cheerful. "Heard the university gave you some unexpected vacation time."

Max sighed. "You could say that."

"Well, look at the bright side—you finally have time to catch up on all those dusty books you love so much."

"Always the optimist," Max replied dryly.

"Listen, a few of us are grabbing drinks tonight at that new place downtown—The Quantum Lounge. You should join us. Might do you some good to get out of that cavern you call a home."

Max hesitated. The thought of loud music and superficial conversation was less than appealing. "Thanks, but I think I'll pass. I've got... things I'm working on."

Chris was silent for a moment. "Still the lone wolf, huh? Suit your-self. But if you change your mind, you know where to find us."

"Appreciate the invite," Max said, though his voice lacked enthusiasm.

"Take care of yourself, Max," Chris added, a hint of genuine concern creeping into his tone before he disconnected.

Max set the phone down, contemplating the brief exchange. Despite their differences, Chris was one of the few people who made an effort to reach out. Perhaps he should make more of an effort himself.

He returned to the painting, but the earlier momentum had faded. Frustrated, he tossed the brush aside. The silence pressed in again, heavier this time. His thoughts circled back to the dagger—the one he'd found during his last expedition. It was an ancient artifact, etched with symbols he hadn't been able to decipher. Since the blackout, he'd felt an inexplicable connection to it.

"Maybe now's a good time," he mused.

Retrieving the dagger from a display case, he sat down at his desk, spreading out reference books and notes. The symbols seemed to dance before his eyes, teasing him with their elusiveness. He traced a finger over the markings, and suddenly, a sharp image flashed in his mind: the woman from his vision standing amidst ruins, the dagger in her hand.

Startled, Max jerked back. His heart raced as he tried to make sense of it. Was his mind playing tricks on him, or was there a deeper connection? He'd always been rational, grounded in logic and science, but recent events were challenging his perceptions of reality.

Determined to uncover the truth, he dove into his research with renewed vigor. Hours passed as he cross-referenced texts, piecing together fragments of history and mythology. Patterns began to emerge—mentions of cosmic events, alignments of stars, and tales of individuals experiencing profound transformations.

A realization struck him: the global blackout wasn't an isolated incident. It was part of something much larger, something that perhaps connected him to others who were experiencing similar phenomena.

He leaned back, rubbing his temples. Exhaustion tugged at him, but so did a flicker of excitement. For the first time in a long while, he felt a sense of purpose beyond the confines of his academic pursuits.

His phone buzzed again, this time with a text message. He glanced at it to see a message from an unknown number: "If you want answers, meet me at the old observatory tomorrow at midnight."

Max stared at the screen, a mix of suspicion and intrigue swirling within him. Who could this be? And how did they know about his quest for answers?

"Well, that's not ominous at all," he muttered.

He weighed his options. It could be a prank or, worse, a trap. But his gut told him otherwise. There was a connection here—a thread pulling him toward something he couldn't ignore.

Resolute, he decided he would go. Standing up, he felt a surge of energy, a clarity that had been absent since his hospital stay. He looked around the loft, the shadows no longer menacing but filled with possibility.

Setting the dagger carefully back into its case, he prepared for what lay ahead. Tomorrow would bring new challenges, but also, perhaps, the answers he so desperately sought.

As he headed toward his bedroom, a faint smile crossed his lips. "Guess I'm doing something after all," he said to himself.

The silence of the loft felt different now—not a cage, but a canvas upon which the next chapter of his life would be painted.

As Maximus reached his bedroom, the spaciousness of the loft did little to quiet the restlessness within him. He moved toward the far wall, his steps measured and deliberate. Placing his hand against a seemingly solid section, he applied firm pressure. With a soft, mechanical sigh, the wall yielded, revealing a hidden entrance that only he knew existed.

Stepping inside, motion-sensor lights flickered to life, casting a muted glow over the secret chamber. The air was cooler here, tinged with the scent of memories long suppressed. In the corner sat a large black chest, its surface smooth and unadorned, yet heavy with unspoken history. Max stared at it for a long moment, his eyes reflecting a mixture of trepidation and longing.

The chest was both a danger and a lifeline—a relic from a past he had tried desperately to bury. It beckoned to him like a siren's call, stirring echoes of a time when his skills were honed for purposes he no longer wished to serve. He could almost feel the weight of it pulling him back into shadows he had fought to escape.

"No," he whispered to himself, his voice barely audible. He didn't want to go there. His life now was about enlightenment—teaching, learning, contributing something meaningful to the world. To enhance life, not to take it away. The man he was now had no place for the tools of who he once had been.

Max shook his head, breaking the spell. He turned away, his decision reaffirmed. As he stepped back into his bedroom, the lights behind him dimmed, casting the secret room into darkness once more. But just before the hidden door closed, he glanced back over his shoulder, his gaze lingering on the black chest.

"Maybe someday," he murmured, acknowledging the unresolved part of himself that the chest represented.

He let the panel slide shut, sealing away the remnants of his past. For now, he would focus on the path ahead—on the mysterious message and the questions it posed. Whatever awaited him at the old observatory, he would face it on his own terms, without the shadows of his former life weighing him down.

Max returned to the main room of his loft, feeling a subtle shift within himself. The silence no longer felt oppressive. Instead, it was filled with possibilities, the beginning of a journey that was both new and eerily familiar. He set down his glass, the bourbon untouched, and allowed himself a faint smile.

Perhaps the answers he sought wouldn't be found in the relics of his past, but in the choices he made moving forward. And with that thought, he headed toward his bed, ready to embrace whatever the night—and the future—might bring.

# CHAPTER
## THIRTEEN

Jose Martinez sat in his room at the Iron Clan hideout, the dim light casting shadows that made the room feel even more confined. His gaze landed on a family picture that had slipped from its usual place on the wall to the floor. Picking it up, Jose held it gently, studying the familiar faces that once filled his life with warmth and laughter. These quiet moments often unlocked the memories he kept buried within, in a place where sorrow and nostalgia mingled painfully.

Each day, the absence of his family gnawed at him. Ever since he turned eighteen, Jose had scoured the city for any sign of his siblings, but each lead fizzled into despair. It had been two years since he last chased a whisper of his youngest brother at a local community center— two long years that had transformed him from a hopeful brother into a hardened member of the Iron Clan, the only family he had left.

Recently, Jose found himself reflecting more on the past, on the faces of the young men and women he had brought into the Assembly, and on the day he met Matt—an encounter that had felt like a twist of fate.

A knock on the door jolted him from his reverie. He carefully placed the picture back on the wall and called out, "Come in."

Mason entered, closing the door softly behind him. His face was etched with concern.

"How are you feeling?" Mason asked, crossing the room to stand beside Jose.

"Better than last week, that's for sure," Jose replied, managing a weak smile despite the weight of recent events.

Mason nodded, his expression grave. "It's been surreal, hasn't it? One minute you're fine, the next it feels like the end is near, and then suddenly, you're feeling better than ever."

"Yeah, I never want to go through that again," Mason confessed, catching the look of conflict that momentarily crossed Jose's face.

"What's on your mind?" he prodded gently.

Jose paced a few steps, his restlessness palpable. "We've just received new orders."

Mason's eyebrows raised in inquiry. "What now?"

With a wave of his hand that betrayed his inner turmoil, Jose replied, "The same as always—cause chaos."

Mason suddenly grasped his hand, flinching from a sudden pain.

"What's wrong?" Jose asked, concern quickly replacing frustration.

"Just a sharp pain... it's been happening on and off. My hands feel like they're burning," Mason explained, bewildered by the sensation.

"That's odd," Jose remarked, trying to inject some humor. "You were burning up in the hospital too. The doctors couldn't believe you pulled through."

"Yeah," Mason chuckled weakly. "Kept hearing them ask how I was still alive."

"So, did the boss specify what kind of chaos?" Jose pressed, eager to steer the conversation away from their ailments.

"Just the usual robberies, carjackings. Keep the fear alive in the city," Mason replied darkly. "I hate how he uses us, hiding behind anonymity."

"We allow it, though," Mason acknowledged, his shoulders slumping.

Jose turned sharply, his irritation flaring. "Exactly. But not for much longer. I swear, the day is coming when we'll make our own choices." He walked back to the family picture, whispering to it, "Don't worry, Mama. I'll make you proud."

Noticing Jose's limp, Mason asked, "Hey, when did you start limping?"

"It's nothing, just a sore leg." Jose motioned towards the couch. "Come on, sit down. Let's talk business."

Mason hesitated before speaking, "What had you so deep in thought? I knocked several times."

Jose sighed, "Just thinking about the beginning, when we first got roped into this life."

"You saved my life that day," Mason said, his voice thick with emotion.

In that quiet room, filled with the ghosts of their past, the two men sat in reflective silence, each pondering the journey that had led them here, under the watchful gaze of the mysterious figures who had changed their lives forever.

IN THE WANING LIGHT OF THE DAY, MATTHEW ANDERSON SAT IN his sleek SUV, the tinted windows concealing his watchful eyes. He was perched like a hawk outside the Boys and Girls Club, waiting for the building to spill out its youthful occupants. Earlier, a directive from Eagle Eye had sharpened his purpose: to recruit fresh faces for the chaos Cosa Nostra intended to unleash.

Matthew, an American conduit for the notorious organization, was no stranger to manipulation. His task was clear—target the vulnerable, those young souls abandoned or orphaned, left adrift by life's cruel tides. His leader believed these were the raw materials needed to forge an army, an army that would crown him as the omnipotent force he was destined to be.

"Hey, kid. Got a minute?" His voice cut through the chill of the evening, snagging the attention of a young man sauntering out of the club.

"Yeah, what's up?" The youth's guard was up, his voice tinged with suspicion.

"Looking for a job?" Matthew's tone was casual, as if job offers were handed out to strangers every day.

"What kind of job?" The youth's interest piqued, his stance relaxed slightly.

"Let's just say my boss is orchestrating some complex operations in the city, and we could use someone like you."

"Operations? What are you, like the CIA?" The kid's laugh was skeptical, his eyebrows arching in amusement.

"Not quite, but trust me, we're just as influential," Matthew countered smoothly, a smile playing on his lips.

"And why exactly would your boss want someone like me?"

Matthew leaned in, lowering his voice as if sharing a state secret. "Because, my friend, we believe in giving people a chance to be part of something bigger. Let's go somewhere more private and discuss the details." He nodded towards his SUV, parked under the fading glow of the streetlamp.

"I guess it couldn't hurt. I'm done here anyway." Shrugging, the young man followed, introducing himself, "I'm Jose."

Matthew's eyes assessed him quickly. "Pleasure to meet you, I'm Matthew."

As they settled into a booth at a nearby diner, the conversation shifted from job details to lighter topics like sports, but Jose's mind was whirling. When Matthew finally laid out the proposition, the allure of quick money flashed before Jose's eyes like a neon sign.

"My boss operates internationally and has plans for expansion here. We need sharp individuals like you to ensure everything goes smoothly."

Matthew's hand dipped into his jacket, pulling out a stack of cash that made Jose's eyes widen. "This could all be yours, depending on how committed you are."

"Wow, that's a lot of cash," Jose remarked, his earlier reservations melting away in the face of potential wealth. "What's the next step?"

Over the next few months, Jose dove headfirst into his role, recruiting for what would become known as the Iron Clan. Under Matthew's guidance, he targeted those most susceptible to their charms—youths longing for belonging, willing to venture into the murky waters of legality for a promise of better futures.

"Now, we're looking for individuals between 18 and 25, available anytime, with few family ties," Matthew had instructed. "People who aren't afraid to get their hands a bit dirty."

Jose's induction into their ranks came swiftly. His first task: a daring heist at a local jewelry store, executed with such precision that even Matthew was impressed.

"You might just be a natural," Matthew had said afterward, clapping Jose on the back.

For the first time in a long time, Jose felt valued, even if by those whose morals were questionable. Yet, each night as he lay in bed, the faces of his family haunted his dreams, reminding him of the line he was all too willing to cross for a semblance of worth and recognition.

# CHAPTER

## FOURTEEN

**M**adison awoke to the warm sun streaming through her window and the inviting smell of bacon drifting into her room. For the first time in what felt like forever, the aroma of breakfast didn't cause her stomach to churn. Now that her cancer was in remission, life was beginning to feel wonderfully normal again—no more debilitating headaches, her hair was returning thick and full, her skin was regaining its healthy glow, and today, a Saturday morning, promised a real breakfast: bacon, eggs, and hash browns instead of the usual quick cereal and fruit.

She leapt from her bed and dashed down the hall to the kitchen.

"Good morning, Sleeping Beauty!" Elizabeth greeted her with a bright smile.

"Good morning, Mommy! How did you sleep?"

"Like a log," Elizabeth said, pulling Madison into a warm hug. "Knowing you're truly healing has lifted a weight off my heart."

"Me too, Mommy. And I'm so glad I don't need that yucky medicine anymore!" Madison said, making a face as she remembered the bitter taste.

Elizabeth laughed and turned back to the stove to flip the sizzling bacon. Just days before, her mind had been haunted by fears of losing her daughter. She had clung to hope, despite the dire predictions from the doctors.

"You thought I was going to die?" Madison's question cut through the cozy morning like a knife.

Elizabeth whirled around, almost sending the skillet clattering to the floor. "What? Why would you say that, sweetheart?"

"Because you just said it," Madison replied, her voice tinged with confusion.

Elizabeth's heart skipped a beat. She had indeed thought those words—had they slipped out? "No, honey, I didn't say anything like that. I wouldn't."

"But Mommy, I heard you. You said you knew I'd be alright, and that those doctors tried to scare you into thinking I wouldn't."

Realization dawned on Elizabeth that she hadn't spoken aloud; Madison had somehow heard her thoughts. How was that possible?

As they pondered this mystery, Elizabeth's hand accidentally hit the skillet handle, sending it tipping dangerously. Reacting with surprising agility, she righted it, catching all the bacon and hot grease with a fluid, almost supernatural movement.

Madison's eyes widened. "Mommy! That was amazing! You moved like a superhero!"

Elizabeth, her own heart pounding from the shock, managed a shaky smile. "Let's not test that theory again. Why don't you get ready for breakfast while I finish up here?"

"Okay!" Madison said, bounding out of the kitchen with a skip.

Once alone, Elizabeth touched the cool counter, trying to steady herself. This past week, her senses had been unusually sharp, her reflexes quick. She could almost sense things before they happened. Was this a lingering effect of the stress, or something more? With a deep breath, she turned her attention back to the breakfast, her mind swirling with questions about what had profoundly changed in their lives.

# CHAPTER

## FIFTEEN

Zaccarie had always prided himself on his ability to control his emotions, wielding them as weapons against his enemies. But lately, he found himself searching for a different kind of power—the power of calm, of inner stillness. Meditation was his chosen path to this elusive state, and he practiced it now, sitting cross-legged in a room filled with lush greenery, smooth stones, and the soothing sound of an artificial waterfall. The gentle cascade of water had become a constant companion ever since he awoke from his mysterious seizure.

His mind, however, was far from serene. He needed time to process the events of the past week: the unsettling meeting in the great hall, the sudden sickness that had brought him to his knees, and the strange awakening that followed three days later. And then there was Laurel. Memories of her had returned with a vengeance, crashing through his thoughts like a storm. It had been so long since she had appeared in his dreams, yet now, she was all he could think about.

He remembered the day she had told him he was going to be a father. It was the happiest he had ever been. It was just one more reason he wanted to spend the rest of his life with the woman who had opened his heart to a world of new possibilities. They had planned to marry the day after graduation, a plan that had since become a distant memory. Laurel had been his saving grace, a calming presence that soothed his turbulent, restless soul. She made him want to be a better man. But all of that changed on that dreadful day when a knock on his dorm room door shattered his world.

"Are you Zaccarie Lorenz?" a police officer had asked.

"Yes, sir. How can I help you?" Zaccarie replied, his heart pounding.

"I'm sorry to have to tell you this, but your fiancée has been killed in a car accident."

The words hit him like a physical blow. He collapsed to the floor, unable to move, unable to believe what he was hearing. They had just been together the night before. He hadn't seen her that day because she had to work.

"But how? Why?" he whispered, struggling to his feet.

"I don't have any details," the officer said, his tone flat and procedural. "You were her emergency contact. They've taken her to the hospital morgue. You'll need to speak with them for more information."

Zaccarie's head spun as he stumbled to his desk to call the hospital. He could hardly comprehend the magnitude of what had happened. He found his way to the morgue, where Laurel's body lay lifeless on a cold, silver slab. She looked so different. The light that had always shone from her, that joy and wonder that was uniquely hers, was gone. Their unborn child—taken before ever drawing a breath, before ever taking a step, before ever meeting their wonderful mother. Zaccarie's heart broke in ways he had never thought possible.

The sound of the waterfall brought him back to the present, pulling him out of his painful reverie. Meditation was impossible today. He needed to focus on the future—on his role as Zaccarie Lorenz, leader of Cosa Nostra.

He was about to orchestrate the most significant undertaking the world had ever known. But something had intervened: the mysterious illness that had struck nearly a third of the world's population.

"Was this coincidence?" he thought.

No, there was no such thing as coincidence. Only providence.

He felt a strange stirring deep within, a sensation that had been growing since his awakening. It moved through him like a current, almost as if something was flowing through his veins, a blueprint trying desperately to reveal itself. He couldn't suppress it; the power within him was too strong to contain.

He opened his eyes and reached out to a flower in front of him. It was as if the flower was calling his name. "Water," he commanded.

Instantly, the flower dissolved into a puddle of liquid.

Zaccarie stood, staring at the wet spot on the floor where the flower had been. "Did I just do that?" he whispered, unsure if he was asking himself or the now-absent flower. Had his words somehow altered its very structure?

Excitement surged through him. He scanned the room, eager to test his newfound abilities. His gaze landed on the stones in the waterfall beside him. This time, he didn't speak; he merely thought. One word echoed in his mind. With a gleam of fascination in his eyes, he watched as one of the stones transformed into metal.

A triumphant laugh burst from his lips. "Providence," he declared, his voice filled with a mix of awe and certainty.

Of course, he had been endowed with this new power. He was the leader of the most powerful secret society in the world. Soon, everyone would know the true strength of Zaccarie Lorenz.

# CHAPTER
## SIXTEEN

Time had been a blur for Ron. Here he sat, back at his dismal job at Lotus and Schultz, computing numbers and generally being bored to death with the mundane day-to-day existence he had been living. He wondered how he could just sit there, especially after everything that had occurred. He had been released from the hospital after being exposed to a mysterious outbreak that had plunged him into a coma, only for him to wake up days later with no symptoms and no pain.

Memories of his childhood dreams of writing flooded his mind as he heard what seemed like a thousand computer keys clacking around him, each typing out the story of their own monotonous lives. If ever there was a sign to change his life, this was it. He loved to write, and if this bizarre experience wouldn't push him to pursue his passion, perhaps nothing would.

Lost in thoughts of drafting his next novel, his reverie was shattered by the piercing voice of his boss, Ms. Butler. She was a rigid, middle-aged woman, the epitome of sternness, who rarely cracked a smile.

"Ron," she began, her voice grating like nails on a chalkboard.

Startled, Ron straightened up. "Good morning, Ms. Butler," he replied, mustering as much cheer as he could.

She wasted no time. "Have you prepared the paperwork for the Miller account?"

"Um, no, Ms. Butler. I just…" Ron started, but she cut him off.

"Ron, do you like working here?"

"Yes, Ms. Butler," he responded quickly, albeit half-heartedly.

"Good, because Lotus and Schultz is a top firm that expects its employees to rise to challenges, not fall short. Do you understand me, Ron?"

"Oh, yes, Ms. Butler. I understand. It would have been done on time, but I was in the hospital all last week. I sent word…"

She interrupted him again, her tone dismissive. "Susan Lutz down the hall went into labor and came back two days later to finish her audit project. Now tell me again: what exactly was wrong with you? What were you dying from that you could not complete your duties?"

Ron gritted his teeth, frustration boiling inside him. "She could probably do that because she was conscious, Ms. Butler. I was unconscious, in a coma, for several days."

She shot him a disapproving look. "Make sure your work is on my desk by five."

Ron smiled tightly, a quiet sense of rebellion stirring within him. "As you wish, Ms. Butler."

As she stalked away, irritation in every step, Ron's coworker popped his head over the cubicle wall. "Man, she's extra feisty today."

Ron sighed, his voice a mixture of resignation and defiance. "I've got to get out of this place. It's slowly ripping the life from me. I used to have fun. Now, it's work, gym, and sleep. Isn't there more to life than this monotony?"

His coworker nodded in agreement. "I barely have time for my girl-friend, and she's not happy about it."

Ron's eyes sparkled with a newfound determination. "I think my days here are numbered. Maybe I should start writing about what happened last week."

His coworker laughed. "Yeah, you and about a billion other people."

"Thanks a lot. I can always count on your support," Ron replied sarcastically, standing to leave.

"I'll be the first one with your book on my shelf," his coworker called after him.

Ron made his way to the vending machines, searching for the energy drink he liked. He inserted the coins, but as the drink clunked down, it got stuck. Frustrated, he shook the machine, and suddenly, a surge of energy pulsed through him, rattling the room like an earthquake.

A fissure ripped open the floor, destroying the vending machines and shattering all the glass. Ron stepped back, his heart racing, shock etched on his face.

He knew intuitively that what he felt wasn't a tremor. Pondering silently, Ron whispered to himself, "What's going on with me?"

Quietly returning to his cubicle, he sat, enveloped in silence, reflecting on the recent surreal events. Each touch seemed to spark a shock, growing stronger by the day. At night, as he gazed at the stars over the ocean, they seemed to whisper secrets of a forgotten childhood and promises of a future full of potential.

Resolved, Ron packed his belongings and walked to the elevator, dropping off the report Ms. Butler had demanded on his way.

He had a date with destiny at the beach.

# CHAPTER

## SEVENTEEN

**M**artinez had recruited his basketball buddy, Mason Stone, from the Boys and Girls Club to be his second in command. The core group also included Daniel Williams, Craig Miller, Adam Taylor, Abby Johnson, Linda Moore, and Joy Davis. Jose and Mason had known some of them from the neighborhood and since childhood. Dubbed misfits, most came from broken homes; others simply felt out of place in the world, typical of many young adults seeking their identity.

They convened in an abandoned house Jose had discovered, a dilapidated two-story on the wrong side of town, symptomatic of the city's neglect due to lack of funds. Enclosed by a nine-foot iron fence, the property featured rotting wood, shattered windows, and a foreclosure sign that clung to the boarded-up front door. Jose had stumbled upon this hideout when he fled his last foster home, where the father was absent, lost to his job, and the mother, a cruel drunk, wielded her belt at the slightest provocation. He had escaped to this forsaken house, finding solace in its neglected corners. Here, he hid for over a year, until he turned 18 and no longer had to dodge the authorities.

Over time, the house had become more than a mere shelter to Jose; it had transformed into a home. He furnished it with discarded items scavenged from dumpsters or left beside trash cans. His long-held dream was to reunite his scattered siblings under this roof, a hope that now seemed more like a fading mirage.

Bringing Mason and the others here felt like assembling a new family. Although they had yet to receive further instructions from their enigmatic benefactor, they began to settle into their chosen rooms, slowly infusing life back into the abandoned structure. One evening, gathered around a makeshift dining table, they debated a name for their fledgling group. Names flew across the room until Jose, inspired by the sturdy iron gate encircling their refuge, suggested "Iron Clan."

"Why that name?" Mason inquired; curiosity piqued.

Jose glanced out the window toward the enclosing gate and responded, "Because iron can be forged into steel, much like us. Now, we're more than just a group; we're a family—a clan."

The name resonated with everyone. "Iron Clan" embodied strength and unity, echoing their collective desire to fight for a place to call their own.

THE NEXT MORNING, A SHARP KNOCK ECHOED THROUGH THE IRON Clan hideout. Mason swung the door open to reveal Matthew Anderson, who appeared tense and hurried. He gestured toward the living room where Jose and the others were gathering.

"Jose, I need to speak with you alone," Matthew said in a gruff voice.

"Come on in, the others are eager to meet you," Jose responded, hoping to foster some camaraderie.

"I don't have time for introductions," Matthew snapped, his impatience clear.

Jose exchanged a glance with Mason, who quickly intervened. "Let's give them some space," he suggested, ushering the group towards the kitchen.

"That was kind of rude," Jose muttered under his breath as he watched his friends retreat.

"I'm not here to make friends, Jose. I'm here to relay orders from the boss," Matthew retorted sharply.

Jose sensed a harshness in Matthew he hadn't encountered before. "I understand, but these are the people you asked me to recruit," he replied, his voice barely above a whisper.

Matthew softened slightly, realizing his brusque manner might have been too harsh. "Look, Jose, I respect what you've achieved here. You've shown initiative and drive—qualities we desperately need. But right now, there's work to do."

"Understood. What's the plan?" Jose asked, motioning to the worn couch. They both sat, the springs creaking under their weight.

Matthew outlined the evening's mission: a break-in across town to steal valuable paintings and jewelry. He then queried about the group's technical skills. "Do you have anyone skilled in cyber-hacking?"

"Abby's our tech expert," Jose answered as Matthew pulled out a small laptop and a stack of files.

"She'll need to use this laptop. These files contain targets that the boss wants... dealt with."

Jose's brow furrowed as he took in the gravity of the task.

"If Abby is as competent as you say, she'll understand what to do with the information provided," Matthew explained, handing over the equipment.

"I'll make sure she starts immediately," Jose assured him.

"Good," Matthew said, clapping Jose on the shoulder. "I have other places to be. We'll speak soon." With that, he left as abruptly as he had arrived.

Jose watched the door close behind Matthew, a mix of apprehension and resolve settling over him. "Well, this just got interesting," he thought to himself, contemplating the new, dangerous path they were about to embark on.

# CHAPTER

## EIGHTEEN

The night air was crisp as Maximus Curton made his way up the winding path to the old observatory. Perched atop a hill overlooking the sleeping city, the once-grand structure now stood as a silent sentinel, its dome silhouetted against the starlit sky. Weeds tangled around its base, and the paint peeled from its walls like memories fading with time. The wind whispered through broken panes, carrying with it the faint creak of rusted equipment abandoned years ago.

Max moved with a stealth born from years of training, his senses heightened. Every rustle of leaves, every distant car horn was cataloged and dismissed. Since waking from the anomaly-induced blackout, he'd felt a resurgence of strength and agility coursing through his veins—a return of the skills he'd tried to leave behind. His footsteps were soundless on the cracked concrete as he approached the entrance, eyes scanning for any signs of a trap.

Inside, the observatory was a labyrinth of shadows. Old telescopes loomed like sentinels in the darkness, and the remnants of scientific endeavors lay scattered—yellowed star charts, obsolete computers covered in dust. Max inhaled deeply, the scent of aged paper and cold metal filling his lungs. His gaze swept the room, noting potential exit points and areas of concealment. If this was an ambush, he intended to be ready.

A faint click echoed—a sound out of place. He tensed, muscles coiled, ears straining. The sharp staccato of heels clicking against the concrete floor grew louder, each step measured and deliberate. From the depths of the shadows emerged a woman, her silhouette gradually illuminated by slivers of moonlight filtering through the shattered windows.

"Eagle Eye," Max uttered, his voice low and edged with disbelief. His face hardened, a quiet anger simmering beneath the surface. "I thought I told you that the next time I saw you, I'd let DeLorenzo finish what he started."

She smirked, that familiar, infuriating curve of her lips that once both captivated and infuriated him. "He can certainly try," she replied, her tone dripping with confidence.

Memories crashed over him—the way her eyes sparkled with mischief, the way she moved like a predator confident in her power. His attraction to her had always been undeniable, a magnetic pull that he'd fought against even before her betrayal.

Max turned sharply on his heel. "I have nothing to say to you."

"You're going to walk away after coming all this way?" Eagle Eye called after him. "Come on, Max, I know you better than that."

He paused, his back to her, taking a steadying breath before turning around. His expression was inscrutable, a mask honed over years of hiding his true feelings.

She raised her hands in a gesture of surrender. "Can we start over?"

"I wish we could," Max said quietly. "I wish we could go back fifteen years to before you betrayed your team—to before you betrayed me. But that's not possible, is it?"

A flicker of something—regret, perhaps—passed over her face. "I'm not here to reopen old wounds. You have your truth, and I have mine."

"Truth?" Max's eyes flashed. "The truth is you left us for dead. I loved you, and you used that against me."

She held his gaze steadily. "You were the best of us, Max. You should have known better."

"But I didn't," he replied bitterly. "And I paid the price."

Silence settled between them, heavy with unspoken words and the weight of shared history. The distant sounds of the city drifted in—a siren wailing, the hum of traffic—a stark contrast to the stillness inside the observatory.

Eagle Eye was the first to break the silence. "How are you feeling?"

Max scoffed, shaking his head. "So that's why I'm here? What scheme are you concocting now?"

"No schemes," she said, taking a cautious step closer. "Full transparency."

He laughed without humor. "You and the truth are as familiar as oil and water. You always have an agenda."

She didn't flinch. "True. But this time, we're on the same side."

He arched an eyebrow. "Since when?"

"Since the anomaly," she replied. "Things have changed, Max. We know you're a part of it."

"We?" His eyes narrowed.

She met his gaze evenly. "The same parties you used to work for—the ones operating behind the veil. Certain government agencies have taken a keen interest. Let's just say they've started... experimenting."

A cold knot formed in Max's stomach. He knew exactly what that meant. Dark projects, ethical lines blurred beyond recognition.

"I'm here to help you," Eagle Eye continued. "The world isn't the same anymore, and they know it. They want to understand why. And the people affected by the anomaly—you included—are at the center of it all."

He crossed his arms over his chest. "That's not my problem."

"It will be when they come after you."

"Let them try," he said flatly, turning away once more.

"And what about everyone else?" Her voice softened, a rare vulnerability creeping in. "I know you, Max. You won't sit by while innocent people are harmed. It's one of your least admirable traits."

He halted, her words hitting their mark. Slowly, he turned back to face her. "I won't be dragged back into that world, Eagle Eye."

"Why? Because you're an upstanding citizen now?" She gestured dismissively. "A scholar in tweed jackets hiding behind stacks of books?"

"I'm a teacher," he replied firmly. "Not a monster."

She took a step closer, eyes piercing into his. "You're a killer," she said, each word deliberate. "And a proficient one at that. No matter how much you deny it, hide from it, or try to bury it under academia—you are who you are, Max."

His jaw tightened. "If that's true, then you should know better than to contact me again."

He turned sharply, striding toward the exit. The echo of his footsteps filled the cavernous space.

"Max!" she called after him, a hint of desperation threading her voice. "You can't run from this!"

He didn't slow, didn't look back. Pushing open the heavy door, he stepped into the cold embrace of the night. The air outside was sharp, filling his lungs and clearing his mind. He descended the worn steps of the observatory, each stride putting distance between him and the ghosts of his past.

Eagle Eye watched him go, a mixture of frustration and something else—something akin to sorrow—etched on her face. She had hoped he would listen, that the man she once knew was still in there, willing to fight for a cause greater than himself.

Max reached his motorcycle parked under a canopy of overgrown trees. As he swung his leg over the seat, he glanced back up at the observatory. For a fleeting moment, he thought he saw her silhouette against the light—a solitary figure amidst the ruins. Then he revved the engine, and the roar drowned out any lingering doubts.

The road stretched ahead, illuminated by the bike's single headlight cutting through the darkness. His mind churned with conflicting emotions. Part of him wanted to forget the encounter, to return to the quiet life he'd built. But another part—a part he tried to suppress—felt the pull of duty, of unfinished business.

"You're not a monster," he muttered to himself, the wind whipping past his face. "Not anymore."

But Eagle Eye's words lingered. Deep down, he knew she was right about one thing: he couldn't ignore the changes happening around him. The world was shifting, and whether he liked it or not, he was connected to it.

As the city lights grew brighter on the horizon, Max made a silent vow. He would protect the innocent, but on his own terms. He would not be a pawn in someone else's game—not again.

For now, he would return to his loft, to the semblance of normalcy he'd carved out. But the encounter had stirred something within him—a restlessness, a sense of impending change.

The night was far from over, and Maximus Curton was a man caught between two worlds, seeking a path that was truly his own.

# PART 2
## A NEW WORLD

CHILDREN OF THE SKIES: DESTINY

# CHAPTER
## NINETEEN

Six months had passed, and the world kept spinning as usual. The group, now known as the Iron Clan, had evolved from petty theft to orchestrating global cyber offenses, hacking into various businesses throughout Los Angeles. The situation escalated to the point where Alexandra Cortez, the Secretary of Homeland Security, was called in for assistance.

The headlines now featured more than just the usual tabloid fodder of Big Foot sightings or the face of Jesus in a cloud. Newspapers, TV screens, and airwaves buzzed with reports of mysterious phenomena that seemed otherworldly and unexplainable. A palpable shift was happening; the boundaries between good and evil, once clear, were now obscured. This new reality wasn't confined to the supernatural—criminal groups like the Iron Clan were part of a burgeoning underbelly that thrived in the chaos.

The chaos wasn't limited to the underworld. The streets of Los Angeles were overwhelmed not only by criminals but also by individuals struggling to come to terms with newfound abilities—a remnant of the mysterious event on May 4th.

The FBI and CIA found themselves outpaced by the rapid escalation of incidents. Each agency received daily tips about crimes committed by individuals with suspicious abilities.

During a press conference, Secretary Cortez addressed the growing crisis. "These criminal activities can be categorized as terrorist attacks. Protecting not only Los Angeles but also cities worldwide has become our top priority. We are committed to finding those responsible," he declared before opening the floor to questions.

"Secretary Cortez, Dylan West from Channel 4 News here. We've received reports from several countries about people developing supernatural powers. Can you confirm the validity of these claims?" Dylan asked, seizing the first question.

Cortez hesitated, her voice betraying his uncertainty. "Mr. West, while we have received similar reports, I cannot comment on their legitimacy at this time. It is part of an ongoing investigation."

Initially skeptical, Dylan found his disbelief eroding as he delved deeper into the rumors and eyewitness accounts of supernatural occurrences.

After the press conference, Cortez met with local law enforcement leaders, including the chief of police and the head of the local FBI office. Unbeknownst to the public—and even his colleagues—Cortez possessed her own abilities and was collaborating with a former covert agent. This agent kept him informed about the Iron Clan and the broader activities of Cosa Nostra.

What Cortez couldn't reveal was that they had obtained video evidence confirming the existence of individuals with extraordinary abilities and were forming a task force to address this new threat. The reality was becoming stranger than fiction, reminiscent of the tales told to children to instill fear.

Cortez grappled with conflicting emotions about his dual life of duty and adventure. His thirst for excitement was at odds with his responsibility to the nation. As the lines between right and wrong blurred, Cortez found herself at a moral crossroads, questioning how far he should go to protect the country he loved.

# CHAPTER

## TWENTY

Maximus Curton stepped into the lecture hall, the familiar scent of chalk and aged books washing over him like a comforting wave. The room was a sanctuary of knowledge, with towering bookcases crammed full of well-worn texts lining the walls, and a massive chalkboard stretching across the front. Sunlight streamed through the tall windows, casting a warm glow on the empty desks that awaited the return of eager minds.

He adjusted the rucksack slung over his shoulder, a faint smile touching his lips at the thought of being back where he belonged. But his smile faltered when he noticed Dean Philips standing near his desk, shuffling papers with a bureaucratic precision. The dean was a meticulous man, always impeccably dressed in a crisp suit that seemed to mirror his rigid personality.

"Dean Philips," Maximus greeted, striving to keep his tone cordial. "Thanks for the welcome."

"Yes, welcome back, Doctor Curton," the dean replied, his voice clipped. "Good to see you. How are you feeling?"

"Better than I've felt in years," Maximus said earnestly, setting his bag down and beginning to unpack his notes.

Dean Philips blinked, momentarily thrown off balance. "Are you sure about that? Perhaps a few more days of rest would be prudent."

Maximus shook his head, a determined glint in his eye. "They ran every test imaginable and found no reason to keep me there. Besides, there are others who need those hospital beds more than I do."

He pulled out a gleaming dagger from his bag, its blade catching the sunlight and reflecting a cascade of light across the room. Dean Philips stared at it, his eyes widening as if he'd just spotted an oasis in the desert.

"I've got it," Maximus said, noticing the dean's gaze fixated on the weapon. "You can't cut me off now. Besides, I think this may have something to do with what happened."

"What do you mean?" the dean asked cautiously.

Maximus paused, choosing his words carefully. "Well, I can't say yet. I'll need to continue my research to find out."

Dean Philips pursed his lips. "I'll be frank, Doctor Curton... Maximus. The board has some concerns about you returning to work so soon. Beyond any lingering health effects, there's renewed press scrutiny to consider."

Maximus met his gaze steadily. "I appreciate their concern, but my health is excellent. Better than I even know."

Absentmindedly, he rubbed his arm through his shirt, where the scars from his past had inexplicably vanished. Before the dean could respond, a familiar voice cut through the air.

"Welcome back from the dead."

Maximus turned to see Christopher Cutty sauntering into the classroom. Young and sharply dressed, Chris had an air of effortless confidence that bordered on arrogance. With a sly grin and eyes that always seemed to be assessing everyone around him, he moved as if the world were his personal stage.

"Good afternoon, Professor Cutty," Maximus replied, a hint of amusement in his tone. "I hope you're doing well."

Chris smirked. "Couldn't be better. I couldn't help but overhear that you're back . I assume there'll be no objections to my return as well, Dean?"

Dean Philips cleared his throat, clearly uncomfortable. "Well, I—"

Maximus raised an eyebrow. "You were affected too?"

Chris shrugged nonchalantly. "Seems so. And like you, I feel fantastic. Unless, of course, there's another reason you might object to me teaching, Max."

Maximus sighed, his patience wearing thin. "I've never had a problem with you teaching, Chris. My concern is with what you get up to outside the classroom."

"Former students," Chris retorted, his eyes gleaming with mischief. "They're adults, capable of making their own decisions."

Dean Philips interjected hastily, "Let's not rehash old discussions. The board has already addressed those matters. As for Professor Curton's return, I'm confident in my decision. Now, if you'll excuse me."

The dean cast one last lingering look at the dagger before making a hasty exit, leaving the two professors alone.

Chris leaned against a desk, crossing his arms. "You know, Max, just because you prefer dusty books over real-life experiences doesn't mean the rest of us have to."

Maximus began arranging his materials, refusing to rise to the bait. "At last, we agree on something—you live your life, and I'll live mine."

"Touché," Chris said with a sly grin. "By the way, what's with the antique?" He nodded toward the dagger.

"Just a piece of history I'm studying," Maximus replied, his tone guarded.

"Always so mysterious," Chris mused. "Well, don't let me keep you from your... thrilling afternoon."

As Chris turned to leave, Maximus couldn't help but feel a mixture of exasperation and fondness. Despite their differences, there was a camaraderie between them—a shared dedication to their fields, even if their approaches were worlds apart.

Left alone in the quiet of the classroom, Maximus approached his bookshelves, his fingers trailing over the spines of countless volumes. He pulled out an old text, but the moment he touched it, a jolt shot through his hand. The book slipped from his grasp, thudding softly against the floor.

"What on earth?" he muttered, shaking his hand. Cautiously, he picked it up again, and as his fingers made contact, a flood of information rushed into his mind. It was as if he'd absorbed the contents of the book in an instant.

He stared at the cover, disbelief etched across his face. Experimentally, he reached for another book. The same sensation—another surge of knowledge seeping directly into his consciousness.

"Oh my God," he whispered, a mixture of awe and exhilaration coursing through him.

From the hallway, Chris watched unnoticed, his brow furrowed as he observed Maximus's peculiar behavior. Seeing his colleague touch book after book with a strange fervor, Chris shook his head, a skeptical smile playing on his lips.

"Always knew he was a bit odd," Chris muttered to himself before strolling away.

Inside the classroom, Maximus was lost in his own world, the possibilities of his newfound ability igniting a spark of excitement he'd not felt in years. The ordeal he'd endured—the blackouts, the mysterious recovery—it was all connected. And now, perhaps, he was beginning to understand how.

He glanced down at the dagger resting on his desk, its polished surface reflecting his contemplative gaze. "Let's see what secrets you hold," he murmured.

As the afternoon light waned, Maximus delved deeper into his research, unaware of the undercurrents of change rippling through his life—and the world—set into motion by forces yet unseen.

# CHAPTER
## TWENTY—ONE

On an unassuming Tuesday morning, Elizabeth Duncan decided to visit the bank before heading to work, favoring the quieter morning hours over the bustling afternoons. As she entered, the guard greeted her with a polite smile, which she returned before joining the end of the queue. Elizabeth appreciated this particular branch, housed in a building from the 1920s, for its cinematic grandeur that always sparked her imagination.

As she stood in line, a few more patrons entered, aligning behind her. Despite the several teller windows, only three were staffed. In front of Elizabeth was an elderly lady, diminutive and gray-haired, who looked like she might spend her days baking apple pies.

"I never understand why they don't have all the tellers here in the morning," the elderly woman lamented, turning to Elizabeth.

"It would be very helpful," Elizabeth agreed, sharing a smile.

"I mean, people are trying to get to work," the woman added.

"It would be nice to just walk in and out," Elizabeth mused.

Just as the elderly woman nodded in agreement, the front door exploded inward, and the wall beside it disintegrated. A powerful droning noise filled the room, causing panic as patrons screamed and ducked for cover. Through the debris, Mason emerged, his hands smoking as if they had been aflame. Elizabeth stared in astonishment, not just at the spectacle but also at Mason's twisted pleasure in his destructive power.

Behind him followed Jose, the leader of the Iron Clan, and two other cohorts.

"Ladies and gentlemen," Jose began, stepping forward. "Please, allow me to introduce myself. You may call me Wax, and these gentlemen are my colleagues. We apologize for the interruption, but if you remain patient, we will soon be on our way."

Craig and Riley, his accomplices, pulled out guns from beneath their jackets, ensuring the patrons' compliance. "These gentlemen will ensure your safety until we return. Please, no cell phones or heroics, and everyone can resume their day shortly."

As Jose and Mason walked towards the bank's vault, Mason whispered with a grin, "That was fun. I feel invincible, like a god or something."

"Focus," Jose hissed back. "Don't get cocky. We're not done yet."

Reaching the vault, Mason readied himself. "Want me to blast it?" he asked eagerly.

"No," Jose instructed firmly. "We need the money unscathed."

Mason's face fell as Jose approached the vault, his physique swelling massively. In moments, he was towering, his shoulders wider than the vault door itself. With the strength of a hundred men, Jose wrenched the vault door off its hinges, revealing stacks of cash inside.

After filling their bags with money, they prepared to leave. "Thank you for your cooperation," Jose announced to the patrons. "We'll be on our way now."

Before they could exit, the elderly woman stood and slapped one of the thugs. The bank fell silent at her audacity.

"Dumb move, grandma," the thug sneered, aiming his gun at her.

In a flash, Elizabeth acted, disarming and incapacitating the gunman with a swift, precise maneuver. She then dodged a fiery blast from Mason, known as Ares, by flipping out of harm's way.

Outside, sirens wailed as police surrounded the bank. "You're surrounded. Come out with your hands up," they announced.

Jose nodded at Mason. "Ares, enough. She's not our concern now. Go handle the cops."

As Mason strode out to confront the police, Jose gave Elizabeth a lingering look, a recognition dawning upon him. "Until we meet again," he said, then disappeared with his crew.

Elizabeth hurried to the elderly woman. "Ma'am, are you alright?"

"Yes, thanks to you," she replied, shaken but unharmed.

As Elizabeth stepped outside, the scene was apocalyptic. Police cars were demolished, officers lay scattered, and the buildings bore the scars of the confrontation. The Iron Clan had vanished, leaving behind only their scorched emblem on the bank's wall—a grim testament to their presence.

# CHAPTER
## TWENTY—TWO

**M**aximus stood in his office, gazing out the window. Over the past few months, his intelligence had increased tenfold; he had absorbed every piece of knowledge from the books he touched. He attributed this newfound ability to the mysterious global event, suspecting he wasn't the only one affected. "Could others be experiencing unique abilities as well?" he mused aloud.

He recalled a recent conversation with Christopher, mentioning that Eric and Lily had also been absent from school around the same time. Lily had been oddly bundled up in two sweaters on a seventy-degree day. Perhaps they, too, had abilities?

Lost in thought, Maximus felt a chill run down his spine as he sensed another presence. Turning, he found a woman standing in his office doorway. "Eagle Eye, what brings you here after all these years?" he asked, his tone guarded.

"I see you still talk to yourself," she teased, stepping into the room. "I thought you'd be happier to see me."

"Happy? The last time we met, you were trying to kill me," Maximus retorted, his voice cool.

"Oh come now, Maximus. I thought we'd moved past that—two old spies like us," Eagle Eye replied, her voice smooth as she approached his desk.

"If you want this meeting to remain cordial, let's avoid dredging up the past," he said, distancing himself slightly by moving his chair back.

Eagle Eye chuckled. "Touchy, aren't we? I'd probably feel the same if I had passed out mysteriously and then discovered new abilities months later."

Maximus raised an eyebrow. "Your knack for knowing everything was always a step ahead, Eagle Eye."

"What can I say?" she shrugged nonchalantly.

"So, what is it that you know?"

"Enough to say that you're not the one asking the questions here," she countered sharply.

Maximus's gaze hardened. "And I know you well enough to understand you wouldn't be here if you didn't need something from me. So, unless you want to find yourself escorted out, I suggest you get to the point."

Eagle Eye's smirk returned. "As much as I enjoy our banter, let's focus on the matter at hand. We can spar later."

"I'm tired of your games, Eagle Eye. You know they always infuriated me."

"Very well. What we understand is that the events of May 4th were no accident."

"And what exactly was it then?"

"We're not sure yet. What we do know is that it affected people differently," she explained, her tone serious. "Some lost consciousness and fell into comas, while others experienced only mild headaches. We believe the severity of the symptoms may be significant."

CHRISTOPHER STOOD OUTSIDE MAXIMUS' OFFICE; HIS HAND pressed against the cool surface of the wall. The muffled voices inside were just audible enough for him to discern the conversation, a skill he had honed over years of eavesdropping on sensitive discussions.

He listened intently as Maximus and Eagle Eye exchanged terse words. Christopher's brow furrowed; the tension in their voices was palpable, each sentence heavy with old grudges and new threats. His concern grew; Eagle Eye was known for her manipulative tactics, and Maximus, despite his newfound abilities, might not yet be a match for her cunning.

As Eagle Eye spoke of the mysterious event of May 4th, Christopher's pulse quickened. He leaned closer to the wall, straining to catch every word. The details were crucial, and his own investigations had hit a wall. Her acknowledgment that the event wasn't a coincidence aligned with his suspicions but hearing her admit it openly was a revelation.

Suddenly, a silence fell inside the room. Christopher's heart skipped a beat, fearing his presence might have been detected. He took a cautious step back, ready to blend into the shadows should either of them exit the office.

Maximus' voice then broke the silence, his tone more inquisitive and less confrontational than before. Christopher's mind raced as he processed the information, piecing together the implications of their words. The severity of symptoms as a significant clue? This was a lead he couldn't ignore.

As the conversation inside ended, Christopher made a mental note to confront Maximus later, away from Eagle Eye's piercing gaze. He needed to understand more about how widespread these abilities were and how they might be harnessed or, more importantly, controlled.

Retreating from the office door, Christopher's gaze was drawn momentarily to his own hands, a subtle tremor visible in his fingers. The realization of his deepening involvement wasn't just professional curiosity anymore; it was personal survival. As he walked away, his mind was already racing with the possibilities and dangers that lay ahead.

MAXIMUS LEANED FORWARD; HIS INTEREST PEAKED BY EAGLE Eye's revelations.

"We know that within three days, everyone who was afflicted had mysteriously recovered as if nothing had happened," she stated matter-of-factly.

"The whole world knows that Eagle Eye. I expected more from you," Maximus retorted, disappointment tinging his tone.

"Does the world know that those who were stricken are now manifesting mystifying abilities?" she snapped back, her eyes narrowing.

Maximus arched an eyebrow and reclined in his chair, intrigued despite himself.

"In upstate New York, a woman can now see through solid objects. In Wisconsin, an old man cultivates crops overnight," Eagle Eye continued, leaning closer.

"What's so special about overnight crop growth?" Maximus asked skeptically.

"He merely has to touch the earth," she clarified.

"Interesting," Maximus murmured, his scientific curiosity piqued.

"We believe others are displaying similar anomalies," Eagle Eye added.

"And what exactly does your team plan to do about this?" Maximus questioned; his tone sharp.

"What do you mean?" she countered.

"You and I both know you've likely seen this as an opportunity rather than a problem," Maximus accused, his gaze piercing.

"Opportunity?" Eagle Eye raised an eyebrow.

"Yes, an opportunity. Imagine what we could learn from this, how it could benefit the world, helping us grow and reach new heights as a species," Maximus said, his voice filled with a rare optimism.

Eagle Eye laughed; a sound devoid of humor. "You're still so idealistic. Benefits? Maximus, take off those rose-colored glasses. Do you really think people with the power to fly or possess superhuman strength will want to assist humankind?"

"Some might exploit their abilities," Maximus conceded, his voice turning somber.

"Exploit is an understatement. Think bigger, Maximus. World domination. If news gets out that humans have developed these powers, can you imagine the chaos? Reporters are already sniffing around the anomalies."

"You want to detain everyone with abilities?" Maximus challenged, his tone hardening.

Eagle Eye paused, her expression unreadable. "Not while I draw breath," Maximus declared emphatically.

"Calm down. I'm not proposing anything extreme. However, we need a contingency for those who might lose control," she reasoned.

"Shifts?" Maximus inquired, a new term catching his attention.

"That's what we're calling them. It seems apt, doesn't it?" Eagle Eye smirked slightly.

"And you envisage a team to manage these Shifts?" Maximus deduced; his interest now fully engaged despite his reservations.

"Precisely. A team led by someone capable, like you," Eagle Eye suggested, her gaze locking with his.

Maximus looked out the window, contemplating. He knew the potential dangers all too well. "Where would my team come from?" he asked, turning back to face her.

"We've identified a few prospects already," Eagle Eye responded, pulling a folder from her briefcase.

She handed him the files. "Start with your own students. Lily Edwards and Eric Mack have shown symptoms."

Maximus skimmed the files. "What am I to tell them? 'Hey, you've got superpowers. Want to help prevent World War III?'"

"Exactly," she said dryly. "There's also Ron Etts. His symptoms were... distinctive."

"How so?"

"He bled excessively. If our theories are correct, his abilities could be extraordinary."

"And where do I find him?" Maximus inquired; his curiosity piqued.

"We'll handle that," Eagle Eye assured. "Think of it, Maximus. Training a new generation of agents."

He sighed, a mix of resignation and excitement. "And the training facility?"

"I'll show you tomorrow. Consider it your new command center," she promised, a trace of the old camaraderie flickering between them.

Maximus knew the stakes were too high to ignore. Despite the complexities of their past, working with Eagle Eye might just be unavoidable.

As she left, Maximus muttered to himself, looking at the last names on the list, Elizabeth, and Madison Duncan, pondering the implications of dragging civilians into their covert world. He turned back to the window, the weight of impending decisions heavy on his shoulders.

# CHAPTER
## TWENTY—THREE

T he Iron Clan was reeling. Despite pulling off a successful heist, the evening had left them feeling more like jesters than feared criminals—all because of one woman, Elizabeth Duncan. Jose remembered her vividly from that night at the hospital, her astonishing speed and agility. It made him wonder: had she too been affected like he and Mason? Did she even comprehend the extent of her abilities? These questions nagged at him as he watched his crew frivolously throw money around as if it were confetti on New Year's Eve, oblivious to the real implications of their actions.

"Alright, everyone, quiet down," Jose commanded, capturing the attention of his crew. They leaned in, eager to hear the plan, their faces a mix of excitement and apprehension.

"Look, this isn't just about payback; it's about clout. We let one person slide today, tomorrow we got a line at our door," Jose explained, pacing back and forth with a palpable intensity.

Mason, always quick to catch the vibe, chimed in, "What's the move, then?"

"We gotta be slick about this. We can't just roll up in there; she'd see it coming a mile away," Jose strategized, his mind racing with potential tactics. "First, we scope her out. Know her moves, her spots, her schedule. When we hit, it won't just be a scare. We're gonna shake up her whole world."

Heads nodded in agreement; the group's earlier frivolity replaced by a more focused energy.

"And what's up with the wallet?" Craig asked, his voice still tinged with irritation from their last encounter.

Jose held up the wallet, a mischievous grin spreading across his face. "This is our golden ticket. We start with her bank accounts, social profiles, all that. We mess with her head until she wishes she never crossed us."

"Yo, Abby, you're on deck," Jose directed his gaze to their tech whiz. Abby, with her sharp eyes and even sharper skills, understood the gravity of her role without a word.

By night, Abby was deep in the digital trenches. Elizabeth's life—an open book for Abby to rewrite. Bank alerts, creepy DMs, and subtle threats wove a net of paranoia and stress around Elizabeth.

Meanwhile, Mason led the physical recon, tracking Elizabeth's daily grind. Their operation was tight, chillingly efficient.

Weeks passed, and the siege on Elizabeth's peace escalated. But Elizabeth wasn't breaking. The clan's digital whispers and shadowy figures only steeled her resolve.

Then, the tipping point came. As dusk fell over the city, Elizabeth left her office, poised and ready. They expected her to be alone, vulnerable. Instead, she was flanked by allies, each touched by the same mysterious event that had empowered Jose and his crew.

The street became a standoff scene right out of a showdown movie. Elizabeth and her unexpected backup faced the Iron Clan, their presence challenging the very notion of power and control in this new, altered world.

Jose and his team, once confident in their dominance, now confronted a mirror image of their own exceptional abilities—other individuals emboldened by the same cosmic twist of fate.

"You guys ready?" Jose murmured to his crew, a rare hint of doubt threading through his voice.

"Let's light this up," Mason replied, his earlier jest replaced by a steely resolve.

But Elizabeth was unfazed. "We're not backing down. Not today, not ever," she declared, her voice ringing clear across the tense air.

As the clash erupted, it was clear that the battle lines were redrawn. No longer just a skirmish in the shadows, this was a public statement: a battle for the soul of a city transformed by chaos and newfound power.

In this reshaped world, where ordinary folks wielded extraordinary abilities, the fight wasn't just about survival—it was about what kind of future they would forge from the chaos of their altered realities.

# CHAPTER
## TWENTY—FOUR

Christopher Cutty hesitated at the threshold of Maximus' office before stepping inside and closing the door with a soft click. He found Maximus standing by the window, gazing out with an air of contemplation.

"Chris, how can I help you?" Maximus asked without turning, sensing his presence.

"I need to confess something to you; actually, a few things," Christopher began, shifting uncomfortably on his feet.

Maximus turned, his expression serious. "Let me guess, it's about the incident with the student."

Christopher looked taken aback. "You know about that? How?"

Maximus waved off the concern. "That's not important right now. What else is on your mind?"

Taking a deep breath, Christopher plunged ahead. "I misled you when you returned from the hospital. I too was affected by that mysterious illness a few months ago."

Maximus straightened, his interest piqued. "Why didn't you tell me earlier?"

"I was scared," Christopher admitted. "I didn't know how you or others would react. And there's more. I overheard your conversation with Eagle Eye."

Maximus' brow furrowed. "Why were you eavesdropping on that discussion?"

"It wasn't intentional at first," Christopher hurried to explain. "But then I learned something crucial about my own condition."

Maximus regarded him for a long moment, then sighed. "Alright, tell me everything. And Chris, this doesn't leave this room."

Christopher nodded, relief washing over him. "The illness changed me. I've developed abilities. I can interact with machines, understand and control them beyond anything I thought possible."

"Incredible," Maximus murmured, absorbing the information. "And dangerous. You realize the implications if anyone else finds out?"

"I do, which is why I came to you. We need to figure out what this means and what we're going to do about it."

Maximus paced briefly, then stopped, looking Christopher directly in the eyes. "First, no more secrets. If we're going to trust each other, it has to be complete. Second, we use this to our advantage."

Christopher nodded eagerly. "I agree. I think we can use my abilities to gather information, maybe even find others who were affected."

"Good. But we move cautiously," Maximus instructed. "For now, keep a low profile. Continue your work and act as if nothing has changed."

"What about Eagle Eye?" Christopher asked, a note of concern in his voice.

"We keep her at arm's length," Maximus decided. "Feed her just enough information to keep her satisfied but nothing substantial. Can you handle that?"

"I can," Christopher confirmed, a determined look settling over his features.

"Excellent," Maximus concluded with a nod. "We're in this together now, Chris. Let's make sure we stay one step ahead."

With a plan forming and their alliance cemented, both men felt a weight lift slightly. They were in uncharted waters, but at least they were not navigating them alone.

As Christopher and Maximus settled into their new understanding, they set about devising a cautious strategy to explore their newfound abilities and the wider implications of the mysterious global event. Over the next few weeks, Christopher delved deeper into his interactions with technology, discovering that his abilities extended beyond mere communication with computers. He found he could manipulate digital data with mere thoughts, subtly altering information without leaving a trace. This ability proved invaluable as they began to gather discreet intelligence on others who might have been affected.

Maximus, meanwhile, took a more direct approach with his own powers, which seemed to focus on knowledge absorption and retention at an extraordinary level. He spent days locked in his office, surrounded by books on genetics, physics, and history, absorbing centuries of knowledge within hours. His mind became a repository of information, which he used to craft strategies to protect themselves and potentially others who were unknowingly thrust into this new reality.

Their efforts were interrupted one evening when Maximus received a cryptic message on his personal phone, a device he thought was secure. The message was simple: "We know what you are doing. Meet us." It was unsigned but carried an air of authority that suggested it could only have come from someone with substantial resources and knowledge.

"This changes things," Maximus muttered to Christopher as they discussed the message in his office.

"It could be a trap," Christopher suggested, his brow furrowed as he considered the possibilities.

"Or it could be an opportunity to learn more about who else knows about the Shifts and what their intentions might be," Maximus countered. "We need more information before we decide how to respond."

Deciding to use Christopher's abilities to trace the message's origin, they discovered it was sent from a server located in a nondescript building in downtown. The building, as they soon found out through further digital sleuthing, was owned by a shell company that itself was tied to a network of other shell companies, masking the true ownership effectively.

"We need to see this place for ourselves," Maximus decided, his voice tinged with the excitement of the hunt. "But we go prepared, expecting a trap."

Armed with discreet body cameras and other surveillance equipment, they approached the building under the cover of darkness. The area was quieter than expected, the building looking abandoned at first glance. However, a faint hum of electricity and the slight buzz of a security camera they spotted at the back entrance suggested otherwise.

Christopher's abilities allowed them to bypass electronic locks and disable security systems with a level of stealth that would be impossible otherwise. Inside, they found a setup that looked less like a corporate office and more like a command center, with monitors displaying feeds from cameras all over the city.

As they explored further, they stumbled upon a small, heavily secured room. Inside, they found a series of documents and a large map with various locations marked, each corresponding to an incident involving individuals with extraordinary abilities.

"It looks like we're not the only ones tracking the Shifts," Maximus noted, examining the documents detailing observed abilities and incidents linked to them.

"This is organized and well-funded," Christopher added, his voice low. "Someone is coordinating a significant operation here."

Before they could delve deeper, the faint sound of footsteps alerted them to the presence of others. Quickly hiding within the shadowed recesses of the room, they watched as several figures entered, discussing the progress of their surveillance and the capture of one of the Shifts.

"We need to get out of here," Maximus whispered, "but we're taking this information with us."

With a plan to expose the operation or use it to their advantage forming, they made their stealthy retreat, minds racing with the implications of their discovery. The world was indeed changing, and now they had a clearer picture of the forces at play, determined to shape the future of the Shifts and the world at large.

# CHAPTER
## TWENTY—FIVE

E lizabeth Duncan's day had wound down into a tranquil evening, the golden hues of sunset casting long shadows through her daughter Madison's room. As she peeked in, Madison snuggled cozily under her blankets, seemingly lost in dreams. The recent kitchen incident, where Madison inadvertently tapped into her mother's thoughts, had left Elizabeth grappling with the possibility that her daughter possessed clairaudience—the ability to discern information through auditory perception beyond the normal range. Elizabeth pondered deeply, knowing sharing this with others might brand her as delusional.

After a few reflective moments, Elizabeth settled beside Madison, brushing her hair gently. "How are you feeling, sweetheart?"

"Really good, Mommy. No headaches or fever today!" Madison replied, her voice vibrant and cheery.

"That's wonderful, honey," Elizabeth smiled, then watched as Madison's expression shifted to curiosity.

"Mommy, were you scared this morning at the bank when you had to fight?" Madison's eyes, wide and earnest, searched her mother's.

Elizabeth paused, masking her surprise. "Why do you ask that, sweetie?"

"I heard what you were thinking," Madison admitted with a small shrug. "I didn't mean to. It just...happens."

Elizabeth sighed, a mix of concern and wonder in her gaze. "Madison, it's important to try to keep to your own thoughts, okay?"

"It's not that easy," Madison confessed. "At school, I hear what the other kids are thinking all the time. Some of their thoughts are...silly."

Elizabeth corrected gently, "Remember what we said about being nice?"

"Sorry, Mommy. It's just hard."

"I know, baby. We'll keep this secret just between us, okay? No one else needs to know for now."

Madison nodded, sealing their promise with a pinky swear, then snuggled down. "Goodnight, Mommy."

"Goodnight, sweetheart," Elizabeth whispered, turning off the lamp.

In the kitchen, Elizabeth poured herself a vodka, the day's events replaying in her mind—the elderly woman at the bank, her own unexpected agility and strength. How was she capable of such feats? She pondered, taking a sip of her drink, her senses still unusually sharp.

The thought was interrupted by a knock. Glancing at the clock—10:30 PM—Elizabeth's brow furrowed. Who could it be at this hour?

As she approached the door, a sudden chill ran down her spine. Madison's scream pierced the silence, "Mommy!"

The door burst open as Elizabeth spun around. Four men charged in. Instinctively, she lunged, positioning herself protectively in front of Madison's room. A sweep of her leg sent the intruders stumbling.

One man quickly regained his footing, but Elizabeth was faster, striking him down with a precise blow. As another attacker lunged with a syringe, she deflected his arm, only to be blindsided by a blunt force to her head. Dazed, she hit the floor.

"Awww, not so tough now, are we?" one attacker taunted, landing a kick to her side.

Through the haze of pain, Elizabeth's mind raced—not just for her own safety, but for Madison's. The reality of their danger was stark, and despite the odds, her resolve hardened. This was no longer just about defending herself—it was about protecting her daughter, whatever it took.

Gritting her teeth against the pain, Elizabeth forced herself up on her elbows, her vision blurry but her determination crystal clear. The man who had kicked her was looming over her, a smirk twisting his features.

"Where's the fight now, huh?" he sneered, leaning down toward her.

But Elizabeth was far from defeated. With a swift, calculated movement, she grabbed his ankle and twisted sharply. He yelped, losing balance and falling to the floor with a heavy thud. Scrambling to her feet, Elizabeth scanned the room—three men were down, but the fourth was charging towards Madison's room.

"No!" Elizabeth's shout filled the room as she launched herself after him. Every fiber of her being was ignited by a primal, protective fury. She tackled him just outside Madison's door, sending them both crashing to the ground.

"Mommy!" Madison's voice was shrill with fear from behind the door.

"It's okay, baby! Stay inside!" Elizabeth called back, struggling to pin down the assailant beneath her.

With a groan, the man pushed against her, but Elizabeth delivered a solid punch to his jaw, stunning him. She then quickly twisted his arm behind his back, subduing him completely. Her breaths were heavy, her body aching, but the adrenaline coursing through her veins made her feel invincible.

Suddenly, the sharp sound of sirens approached, and blue lights flashed through the windows. Elizabeth kept her grip firm on the man beneath her as she tried to calm her racing heart.

Police burst through the already broken door, guns drawn. "Police! Hands where we can see them!"

"I'm not the one you want," Elizabeth gasped, easing off the man as officers moved in, handcuffing him and his groaning companions.

As the immediate threat was neutralized, Elizabeth rushed to Madison's room, throwing open the door. Madison was curled up in her bed, wide-eyed and trembling.

"Mommy, I was so scared," Madison whimpered as Elizabeth scooped her up, holding her tightly.

"It's over now, I've got you," Elizabeth reassured her, feeling Madison's small arms cling to her.

One of the officers approached Elizabeth, a young woman with a concerned expression. "Ma'am, are you and the child alright? Can you tell us what happened?"

As Elizabeth explained, the officer took notes, nodding solemnly. The realization that they had been targeted because of her actions at the bank dawned on Elizabeth—her newfound abilities had drawn dangerous attention, putting both her and her daughter at risk.

After the police had taken their statements and the intruders were carted away, the officer lingered. "We'll need to ensure your safety. There's clearly more going on here."

Elizabeth nodded, her mind racing with the implications. As the officer left, promising to dispatch a unit to watch over their home, Elizabeth looked down at Madison, her resolve hardening. This event had unveiled a stark reality—there were others out there, perhaps with abilities like hers, embroiled in conflicts they barely understood.

"Mommy, are they coming back?" Madison's small voice broke through her thoughts.

"I won't let anything happen to you," Elizabeth promised, a fierce glint in her eyes. Whatever this new world had in store, she would face it head-on, protecting her daughter at all costs.

As the night deepened and Madison finally fell asleep, Elizabeth sat by her window, watching the quiet street. The world had changed, and so had she. Now, more than ever, she needed answers—and she would start by finding out just how deep this rabbit hole went.

# CHAPTER
## TWENTY—SIX

Maximus and Christopher surveyed the scene at Elizabeth's apartment with mounting apprehension. The door, hanging off its hinges, suggested a violent entry. They stepped cautiously over the threshold, alert to any signs of danger or further disruption within.

"Looks like we're too late for subtleties," Christopher muttered as they moved deeper into the apartment, taking in the chaos. The living room was a testament to a struggle, with overturned furniture and personal items scattered across the floor.

As they approached the hallway leading to the bedrooms, Maximus's sharp senses caught a faint noise—a mix of whispers and a subtle metallic clink. He signaled to Christopher, and they paused, listening intently. It was coming from the back room. Without a word, they communicated through gestures honed by years of working together, and advanced with careful synchrony.

MAXIMUS AND CHRISTOPHER STOOD IN THE DISHEVELED LIVING room, assessing the scene. Madison's raw display of power left them both uneasy but also confirmed the urgent need for their intervention.

Elizabeth groaned as another blow landed, the force sending shivers through her body. From the doorway, Madison, witnessing her mother's suffering, screamed in a voice far too powerful for her small frame, "Leave her alone!"

The intruders paused, chuckling at the child's command, but their laughter was abruptly cut short. One of the men froze, his body rigid as if caught in an unseen grasp. The remaining three turned back to Madison, who stood with an eerie calm, eyes glowing like twin moons.

"Help my mother up," Madison commanded in a tone that brooked no refusal.

To Elizabeth's astonishment, the man obeyed, gently lifting her to her feet. She steadied herself, her eyes never leaving her daughter.

Madison's voice, chilling and decisive, followed, "Now, hit your heads against the wall until you bleed."

Compelled by the young girl's formidable will, the men began to obey, thudding their heads against the plaster with disturbing obedience. Maximus and Christopher burst through the door at that moment, taking in the bizarre tableau.

"Madison, stop!" Elizabeth cried, rushing to her daughter's side in an attempt to snap her out of her trance.

Christopher quipped amidst the chaos, "That's not something you see every day."

As Madison turned to face the newcomers, the ominous glow from her eyes began to wane.

"We're here to help," Maximus assured, raising his hands in a peaceful gesture. "We saw your door was open."

"He's telling the truth," Madison confirmed, the light in her eyes fading completely.

Maximus knelt beside the unconscious men. "I'll handle this," he assured, pulling out his phone to make a call.

Elizabeth, still processing the events, demanded, "Who are you calling? And who exactly are you?"

"Just people who will understand and can manage this situation properly," Maximus replied without looking up from his phone.

"That my daughter can manipulate minds?" Elizabeth pressed, skepticism lacing her tone.

"Yes," Maximus affirmed. "That's precisely why we're here."

Christopher stepped closer, trying to ease the tension. "We're like you. We have special abilities too."

Curious despite the situation, Madison asked, "Like what?"

"I can communicate with computers," Christopher explained, attempting a reassuring smile.

The explanation did little to clear the confusion. "You talk to them?" Elizabeth asked, her tone a mix of incredulity and intrigue.

Maximus pocketed his phone and approached. "The situation is handled. Now, we really need to get you both to safety."

"And just who are you?" Elizabeth insisted, her arms crossing as she guarded Madison.

"I'm Maximus Curton, a professor at UCLA, and this is Christopher Cutty, my colleague. We're here to help because of your abilities. I promise more explanations on the way, but we need to move now."

Madison tugged at Elizabeth's hand. "He's telling the truth, Mommy."

After a tense pause, Elizabeth nodded. "Get what you can quickly," she instructed Madison, who darted away to pack.

When they regrouped, the small party moved toward the door, stepping into the cool night air. Maximus cast one last glance back at the darkened apartment, a weight settling on his shoulders as they walked into the unknown.

# CHAPTER
## TWENTY—SEVEN

Ron found himself, as usual, heading towards the beach to reflect over the day's events. In the last six months, little had changed. The irritation stirred by his miserable boss, Ms. Butler, could only be quelled by savoring a candy bar—his little escape in an environment devoid of pleasure. The incident at the vending machine still played vividly in his mind; it had jammed, and something inside him had snapped. Next thing he knew, a fissure had cracked open the floor, running up the wall from where he stood.

He was still grappling with the reality of what he had done. Daily, Ron pondered, "How is any of this possible?"

All he knew was that whenever he got riled up, usually by Ms. Butler, an energy surge radiated within him. He wasn't sure if anyone had seen him that day; no one had ever mentioned it, but moments of fear haunted him nonetheless.

The ocean was Ron's sanctuary, the best place to clear his head and gain a fresh perspective on the overpowering emotions. As he strolled along the sidewalk near the pier, watching the sun retreat from the world, a disturbance caught his attention. Ahead, three teenagers were being chased by a police officer; it seemed the drama never ceased for him these days.

Ron paused, watching the pursuit head in his direction. Unsure of what to do next, he simply observed. As the teens neared, he saw one of them open his mouth and release a gust of wind, blowing sand into the officer's face and momentarily stunning him.

Did he really just see that? Had the kid truly blown air from his mouth? The officer quickly recovered and reached into his holster, pulling out a Taser.

Ron felt as if he were in a dream.

What had these teens done to warrant such a chase? Was it because the officer had seen them use whatever unique skill Ron had just witnessed? The teens were now just a few feet away. Ron's pulse quickened, his temperature rose, and the familiar rage began to build, threatening to become uncontrollable, just like when the fissure had appeared.

The officer issued his final warning as the teens neared Ron's side. "Freeze! I will not hesitate to use force," he yelled, raising his hand to release the Taser's cable at the young girl trailing behind the others.

Suddenly, before Ron could think better of it, he lifted his hands and released an invisible force that threw the officer several feet backwards, knocking him unconscious. The teens stopped to gawk at the spectacle.

"Wow! Did you guys see that?" the girl exclaimed, amazed.

The tallest boy, with long black hair and a muscular build that made him appear older than his age, responded, "Thanks, man. He would have busted us for sure."

The other boy, with short dirty-blonde hair who had produced the wind, chimed in, "We need to bring him with us. Just imagine what Jose will say."

"Okay," agreed the tall boy, after a quick nod from the girl. "You should definitely come with us."

"Go with you where?" Ron asked, his curiosity piqued.

"With friends," the girl replied, approaching Ron. "To the others just like us."

"Besides, he'll be waking up soon, and you don't want to be here when he does," the blond boy said, nodding toward the officer on the ground. With that, all three teens, with Ron in tow, disappeared into the streets of Venice.

# CHAPTER
## TWENTY—EIGHT

Maximus, along with Christopher, Elizabeth, and Madison, arrived at his suburban home. The house, reminiscent of 1920s and 1930s architecture, struck Elizabeth as charming and reassuring despite Maximus being a stranger. He led them to the living room where Elizabeth and Madison sank into the couch, their adrenaline subsiding from the intense past half hour.

"Would either of you care for something to drink?" Maximus inquired, his gaze settling on the mother and daughter.

"Yeah, I would love something. It's been a crazy day," Christopher responded, standing behind the sofa.

Maximus offered him a wry smile.

"No, I'm good," Elizabeth declined.

Before she could speak further, Madison chimed in, "Do you have any orange juice?"

"Small or large?" Maximus asked, a smile playing on his lips.

"Large please," Madison exclaimed.

"Um, a small glass please," Elizabeth interjected. "It's late, and I don't want you up all night looking for the bathroom."

"Small glass, coming right up," Maximus confirmed, then left the room.

Christopher shifted to stand in front of the couch. "Any idea why those thugs were targeting you and your daughter?"

"We were at the bank this morning when a group of men stormed in and held us hostage," Elizabeth explained.

Maximus reentered with a small glass of orange juice for Madison.

"Elizabeth was just explaining why four psychotic Shifts might be trying to kill her," he said as he handed Madison her drink.

"Shifts?" Madison looked puzzled.

"It's a long story," Christopher replied. "Please continue, Elizabeth."

"As I was saying," Elizabeth resumed, "this morning at the bank, a group of men blasted through the front door. They held us hostage while raiding the vault. It was terrifying how one man could shoot fire from his hands and another grew in size to rip the vault door right off its hinges."

As Elizabeth recounted the events, Maximus and Christopher exchanged a knowing look.

"Then, as they were about to leave, an elderly woman slapped one of the men. He aimed a gun at her and—"

Madison excitedly cut in, "Mommie went all Bruce Lee on him!"

"Well, I wouldn't say Bruce Lee," Elizabeth moderated, "but I did stop him. They didn't take that well. It wasn't until I got home that I realized my wallet was missing. They must have taken it when it fell out during the scuffle."

Maximus looked at Christopher, concern etched on his face. "Eagle Eye warned it might come to this—Shifts abusing their powers. The situation is likely to escalate."

"Unless what?" Elizabeth prompted.

Maximus leaned in, his voice low. "Before we discuss that, may I ask what exactly you can do?"

"My reflexes are beyond normal; I can move with inhuman speed and react instantly, even though I've never had martial arts training," Elizabeth shared.

Turning to Madison, who was finishing her juice, Maximus asked, "And you, Madison? Your abilities relate to the mind?"

"It's okay," Elizabeth reassured her daughter, who then opened up.

"I can hear thoughts and tell people what to do. Oh, and I can move things with my mind," Madison declared proudly.

"Incredible," Christopher exclaimed.

Standing, Elizabeth challenged, "Since we've shared, how about you?"

"I absorb knowledge from any book I touch," Maximus revealed.

"And I'm sort of a human-machine hybrid," Christopher added with a grin.

Elizabeth frowned. "How did you know to find us? You didn't just stumble upon us."

"We were informed you and Madison were Shifts—that's the term the government uses for people like us," Christopher explained. "After the infection spread globally, those affected gained various abilities. The government knows and is monitoring this."

Maximus continued, "I'm assembling a task force to counteract those Shifts who misuse their powers."

Elizabeth laughed softly, incredulous. "You want to recruit us? I'm an editor, and my daughter is just a child. How can we fight against people with such dangerous powers?"

"I'll train you," Maximus assured. "I used to work for the government in a capacity that required a particular set of skills. Trust is essential here."

"Trust you? We're leaving," Elizabeth said, heading for the door with Madison.

Christopher quickly interjected, "You're in danger. Those men won't stop. We can protect you and teach Madison to control her powers."

Pausing at the door, Elizabeth considered their predicament. The realization that fleeing might put them in even greater danger prompted her to reconsider.

"What should we do?" she asked, uncertainty coloring her voice as she weighed their limited options.

# CHAPTER
## TWENTY—NINE

E agle Eye walked into the great hall of the Greek fortress, unaware of what she was about to encounter. Formerly a museum filled with Greek and Italian artifacts, the space now displayed a bizarre chaos of manipulated materials, unlike anything she had seen before.

"Exactly what has happened here?" she wondered, finding herself momentarily speechless.

As Eagle Eye advanced further into the room for a closer inspection of the disorder, she could swear she saw a human figure melded into the wall, as if the person and the wall were fused. Regaining her composure, she called out tentatively.

"Zaccarie? Zaccarie...?"

A malevolent voice broke the chilling silence.

"I am here."

Eagle Eye, a veteran of countless dangerous missions, felt a real fear clutch at her heart for the first time. Here, in this room, knowing Zaccarie possessed an ability to manipulate matter, she was genuinely frightened.

"Where?"

A sinister laugh echoed around her.

"Here..."

"Enough games, Zaccarie. Reveal yourself," she demanded.

The wall to her left began to distort as the stone shifted, gradually forming the silhouette of a human figure. Zaccarie emerged with a mischievous grin.

"Boo," he said lightly.

"Interesting trick," Eagle Eye replied, her heart rate slowly returning to normal as she tried to maintain her composure.

"I've been perfecting my gift while you were away. Please, have a seat," Zaccarie gestured grandly.

Eagle Eye looked around, skeptical of sitting, then back at Zaccarie, "Where?"

Zaccarie raised his hand, and the stone beneath her feet liquefied, forming a chair right where she stood. In awe, she watched as he replicated the process for himself.

"Enjoying your newfound capabilities?" she inquired cautiously.

"Actually, I am," Zaccarie confessed, settling into his stone chair. "While honing my powers, I began to think. Cosa Nostra has long prepared the path for a One World Order using tools like disease, racism, poverty, and economics—tools designed to manipulate mankind through fear."

"What's changed? Everything was in place. What is this new realization?" she questioned.

"I no longer need those crude tools to lead Cosa Nostra or to establish a One World Order. I am the new One World Order, and I alone will be its ruler."

"Cosa Nostra will never allow this," she countered.

Zaccarie stood abruptly, his expression darkening as he left his chair in a pile of rubble. "I am Cosa Nostra!" he declared with fierce pride.

"You know as well as I do that they will try to stop you."

"They will try, but they will not succeed," he asserted with confidence.

"Then why not use them to your advantage instead of revealing yourself so early? Let them take the fall, then begin your ascension quietly."

Zaccarie paced the room, contemplating her devious proposal.

"Intriguing thought. You really can be cunning, my dear," he acknowledged.

"You have no idea," she replied, a devilish tone coloring her voice.

"I will give it further thought."

"There's one more matter," she continued.

"Which is?"

"A task force is forming in the United States to combat Shifts who misuse their powers."

"Really, where?"

"The United States. And you'll never guess who their leader is."

"Who?"

"Maximus Curton," Eagle Eye revealed slowly, watching for his reaction.

Zaccarie's interest piqued significantly at the mention.

"Maximus, oh Maximus..."

"I thought that might pique your interest," Eagle Eye added with a knowing look.

"Why, of course it does, my dear. Maximus always strived to do what's right. I wouldn't have expected anything less," Zaccarie responded, a trace of worry in his tone. "Keep your eyes on him—no pun intended—and keep me updated on their progress," he instructed as he gazed out the window, lost in thoughts of the man he once knew well, the man with whom he had once shared a dorm room.

"Professor Curton...it's been so long..." He murmured, his eyes alight with a mix of nostalgia and malice. "Oh, my dear Maximus, I have a nice surprise for you."

# CHAPTER
## THIRTY

E agle Eye cautiously stepped into the great hall of the Greek fortress, a structure that once housed a prized collection of Greek and Italian artifacts. Now, it presented a disturbing scene of chaos and alteration, as if reality itself had been maliciously twisted. The room was unrecognizable, filled with warped materials and objects reshaped by an unseen force. Eagle Eye's trained eyes scanned the surroundings in disbelief, pausing as she thought she discerned a human figure melded disturbingly into the wall.

"What on earth happened here?" she whispered, her voice barely audible in the eerie silence.

As she ventured deeper, her attempts to process the scene were interrupted by a sudden, malevolent whisper that sliced through the quiet.

"I am here," it declared ominously.

Eagle Eye, who had faced countless dangers in her career, felt a chill run down her spine. It was the first time she genuinely feared for her life, knowing Zaccarie's newfound ability to manipulate matter itself was beyond any threat she had previously encountered.

"Where are you?" she called out, trying to steady her voice.

Laughter, cold and mocking, echoed around her.

"Here..."

"Enough with your games, Zaccarie. Show yourself," she demanded, steadying her nerves.

In response, the wall to her left began to undulate. The solid stone appeared to melt and reshape, eventually forming the distinct silhouette of a man. Zaccarie materialized from the wall with a smirk that chilled her to the bone.

"Boo," he taunted, amusement flickering in his eyes.

"Quite the party trick," Eagle Eye responded dryly, her pulse slowly stabilizing.

"I've mastered my gift in your absence," Zaccarie boasted, gesturing for her to sit. "Please, take a seat."

Looking around warily, Eagle Eye saw no chairs, only the manipulated stone. At his gesture, the floor beneath her softened and morphed into a seat. Astonished yet intrigued, she watched as Zaccarie replicated the phenomenon for himself, and they both sat facing each other.

"So, you're enjoying your monstrous capabilities?" she probed cautiously.

"Immensely," Zaccarie confessed with a twisted grin. "While refining my powers, I contemplated the legacy of Cosa Nostra and our centuries-old ambition for a One World Order. Traditionally, we've manipulated through fear—using disease, discrimination, poverty, and economic crises as our tools."

"And what's led to this sudden epiphany?" Eagle Eye pressed, sensing more to his revelation.

"My ambitions have evolved," Zaccarie stated flatly. "The old tools are obsolete. I no longer need Cosa Nostra to herald the dawn of a new world order—I am that new order, and I shall rule it alone."

"That's a betrayal Cosa Nostra won't tolerate," she countered sharply.

Zaccarie rose abruptly, his form menacing. "I am Cosa Nostra now," he declared, his voice echoing off the stone walls.

"But they will resist you," Eagle Eye argued, undeterred by his intimidation.

"They might try, but they will fail," he asserted with cold certainty.

"Why not manipulate them to your advantage? Keep your machinations hidden until you're ready to seize power unchallenged."

Pacing with predatory grace, Zaccarie considered her cunning suggestion. "You always had a devious mind," he admitted grudgingly.

"And you've barely scratched the surface," she retorted, her voice tinged with dark humor.

"I'll consider your advice," he conceded after a moment.

"There's more," she added. "A new development. A task force is being formed to combat those like us who abuse their powers."

"Where?" he demanded, his interest piqued.

"In the United States. And the leader is none other than Maximus Curton," she revealed deliberately, watching his reaction closely.

The name visibly shook him. "Maximus..." he murmured, a complex blend of respect and rivalry surfacing.

"Thought you'd like to know," she added with a smirk.

"Indeed, it does intrigue me. Keep an eye on him for me," Zaccarie instructed, his thoughts now racing with possibilities. "He was always the moral compass, wasn't he? It's fitting he would oppose us."

"Consider it done," Eagle Eye confirmed, aware of the stakes involved.

As they discussed strategies and potential threats, the twisted game of power and survival continued to unfold, with each player hiding cards yet to be revealed.

# CHAPTER
## THIRTY—ONE

The crisp morning air wafted through the open window into the living room. Maximus, lost in thought, briefly wondered if the previous day's events were just a dream, but the distant snoring of Christopher snapped him back to reality.

He wandered into the kitchen to make a pot of coffee, feeling today called for more than just a single cup. As he was about to take his first sip, a knock at the door echoed through the house. Glancing at the clock which read 8:00 AM, Maximus headed to answer it, assuming the noise had already roused the others.

Peering through the peephole, he recognized the woman on the other side and opened the door to find Eagle Eye, looking impeccably polished even at this early hour. "Why, Maximus, I was hoping to catch you in your pajamas."

"I don't wear pajamas."

"Exactly..." she quipped with a smirk.

Maximus rolled his eyes and stepped aside, allowing her to enter. "What now?" he muttered as he returned to his coffee.

"Interrupted your morning ritual, have I?" Eagle Eye remarked, noticing his annoyance.

"That you have," Maximus replied dryly, his tone flat.

"And here I thought you'd be more welcoming," she teased, her voice dripping with faux disappointment.

Their banter was cut short by the arrival of Christopher, who sauntered into the kitchen. "Oh, my bad, didn't mean to interrupt your tête-à-tête with Ms. Hottie," he remarked, shooting a playful glance at Eagle Eye.

"Christopher Cutty," Eagle Eye responded coolly, her gaze shifting between him and Maximus. "You weren't in our files. Perhaps an oversight we should rectify?"

"Or perhaps we could discuss it over breakfast?" Christopher suggested, his tone suave.

Eagle Eye gave him a measured look. "Many have tried to charm their way, Mr. Cutty. Only one has ever succeeded."

"I like my odds today," Christopher quipped, unfazed.

Maximus, finally taking a sip of his coffee, interjected, "Enough, both of you. Eagle, stop baiting him. And Chris, trust me, she's more trouble than you want."

"Maximus, such harsh words," Eagle Eye feigned hurt.

"I only wish they weren't true..." Maximus muttered under his breath.

Just then, Elizabeth and Madison descended the stairs, drawn by the noise.

"Morning, Chris! Morning, Maximus!" Madison greeted them cheerfully.

"Good morning, Madison," Maximus responded with a warm smile.

"Who is this?" Elizabeth murmured to Maximus as she eyed the unfamiliar woman.

"I'm Eagle Eye, here to assist," Eagle Eye introduced herself formally, her tone professional yet friendly.

Elizabeth exchanged a skeptical look with Maximus. "And how exactly do you plan to help?" she asked, her tone laced with caution.

"Trust is optional; cooperation isn't," Eagle Eye replied sharply. "Now that we're all acquainted, I suggest we prepare for a little excursion. Get dressed, everyone. We're taking a trip."

"And where might that be?" Maximus inquired, as the group's curiosity peaked.

"To the Parthenon," Eagle Eye announced, her smirk hinting at the significance of the destination.

With a mix of intrigue and apprehension, the group hurried to ready themselves, each person pondering what awaited them at such a historic and symbolic site.

# CHAPTER
## THIRTY—TWO

As the crisp morning breeze drifted through the open window, Maximus found himself pondering whether the tumult of the previous day had been nothing more than a dream. However, the distant sound of Christopher's snoring dispelled that notion.

Making his way to the kitchen for his morning ritual of coffee, Maximus considered the magnitude of tasks ahead. Deciding a single cup wouldn't suffice, he prepared to down the entire pot. Yet, before the warm liquid could grace his lips, a persistent knocking at the door halted him. Checking the time—8:00 AM—he figured the rest of the house must be awake by now.

Approaching the door, Maximus peeked through the peephole and immediately recognized the visitor. Opening the door, he was greeted by Eagle Eye, impeccably dressed and flashing a playful smile. "Why Maximus, I was hoping to catch you still in your bedclothes."

"I don't wear bedclothes," he retorted dryly.

"Exactly..." Eagle Eye quipped, stepping inside.

Maximus sighed, stepping back to let her in. "What brings you here at this hour?" he inquired as he resumed his path to the kitchen.

"Interrupting your coffee? My apologies," she remarked, noticing his unfinished task.

Maximus finally took a sip of his coffee, then set the mug down with a clank. "Eagle Eye, if you're here, it must be important. So, what's the urgency?"

Her demeanor shifted to a more serious tone. "It's about the operation. Things are escalating faster than we anticipated."

Maximus's interest piqued. "Do elaborate."

Eagle Eye leaned against the kitchen counter, her expression grave. "The shifts in power dynamics we've been monitoring? They're not isolated incidents. There's a pattern emerging, and it's painting a disturbing picture."

Maximus frowned, processing the information. "You mean the incidents involving the Shifts?"

"Exactly. It's becoming clear that these are not random outbreaks of power. Someone is orchestrating these events, manipulating these individuals for a larger agenda."

The gravity of her words hung in the air as Maximus absorbed the implications. "This goes deeper than random acts of violence..."

Eagle Eye nodded solemnly. "Much deeper. And I fear if we don't unravel this soon, we may be facing a crisis that could spiral out of control."

Maximus's gaze hardened, his resolve firming. "Then we'll need to accelerate our efforts. Gather all the intel we have. It's time we called in every resource at our disposal."

Eagle Eye's expression softened, a rare hint of admiration flickering in her eyes. "I knew I could count on you, Maximus. I'll coordinate with the teams and ensure we have a comprehensive strategy session later today."

"Good. Keep me updated, and Eagle—be careful. We're treading into dangerous waters."

With a nod of acknowledgment, Eagle Eye turned to leave, her steps resolute. Maximus watched her exit, the weight of their impending challenges settling in. Turning back to his coffee, he took a deep sip, steeling himself for the day ahead. The game was on, and the stakes were higher than ever.

# CHAPTER
## THIRTY—THREE

The cool morning air swept into the living room through the open window, shattering Maximus' fleeting hope that the previous day's events were just a dream. Christopher's distant snoring was a jarring reminder of reality.

Maximus shuffled into the kitchen, his mind racing with the tasks ahead. He decided a whole pot of coffee was necessary today. He was about to sip his freshly poured cup when a knock at the door halted him. Glancing at the clock, which read 8:00, he walked to the door, the doorbell chiming as he moved. He peeked through the peephole and immediately recognized the woman outside. Opening the door, he was greeted by Eagle Eye, looking impeccable even at this early hour. "Why Maximus, I was hoping you'd have your bed clothes on," she teased.

"I don't wear bed clothes," Maximus retorted dryly.

"Exactly..." she smirked, stepping past him into the house.

Maximus rolled his eyes and followed her back to the kitchen, his irritation palpable. "Now what?"

"Did you have your coffee this morning?" she inquired, a playful tone in her voice.

"Actually, no, you interrupted my daily ritual."

"That explains your lack of enthusiasm," she quipped, winking.

"Oh, I just hate to spoil this little game for you, Eagle Eye, but I'm not playing today, and I have a lot to do," Maximus shot back.

Their banter was cut short as Christopher stumbled into the kitchen, rubbing his eyes. "Oh, my bad, I didn't mean to interrupt you and Ms. Hottie," he said, giving Eagle Eye a suggestive look.

"Christopher Cutty," Eagle Eye responded sharply, her tone cooling. "We didn't have you in our files, but perhaps we should," she added, her gaze flicking to Maximus with a pointed look.

"Well, how about we go grab a bite to eat, and I can debrief you?" Christopher suggested, his tone dripping with innuendo.

Eagle Eye turned to face him squarely. Maximus, seizing the moment, finally took a sip of his coffee.

"Are you sure you want to try, Mr. Cutty? Many have tried, but only one has succeeded," she challenged.

"Oh, I'm feeling pretty lucky these days," Christopher replied with a grin.

Maximus intervened. "Enough, you two. Eagle, stop provoking him. And Chris, this woman is like Chinese water torture in human form. You want nothing to do with that."

"Maximus, you wound me," Eagle Eye responded with feigned hurt.

"I wish I could..." Maximus muttered under his breath.

Just then, Elizabeth and Madison descended the stairs, drawn by the noise.

"Ah, good morning, you two," Christopher greeted them cheerfully.

"Hey, Chris! Hey, Maximus!" Madison chirped, full of energy.

"Good morning, Madison," Maximus replied with a smile.

"Good morning, everyone," Elizabeth added, eyeing the unfamiliar woman in their midst. She leaned closer to Maximus, whispering, "Who is this?"

"Good morning, ladies. My name is Eagle Eye, and I am here to help," Eagle Eye introduced herself with a confident flair.

"There seems to be a lot of that going around. Exactly how are you going to help us?" Elizabeth asked skeptically, her tone edging with distrust.

"You hear that, Eagle? She's suspicious of you... imagine that?" Maximus teased, sharing a knowing glance with Elizabeth.

Eagle Eye caught the glance and smirked. "I do not require your trust, only your compliance. Now that we are all here, everyone get dressed. Let's take a ride," she commanded, turning to leave the kitchen.

"Where to?" Maximus called after her.

Eagle Eye paused at the doorway, a mischievous smile playing on her lips. "To the Parthenon."

The group exchanged puzzled glances before following Eagle Eye out of the kitchen and to their vehicles. The journey was quiet, each lost in their thoughts about the unfolding mystery and what lay ahead at the Parthenon.

Arriving at their destination, the building's austere exterior belied its significant importance. As they entered, the ambiance shifted palpably; the air charged with a blend of ancient dignity and modern secrecy. Eagle Eye led them through a series of corridors, each turn and doorway meticulously designed to blend the old with the new.

"Here we are," Eagle Eye announced as they approached a massive set of bronze doors embossed with intricate Greek patterns. "The heart of Parthenon."

She pressed her palm against a discreetly placed biometric scanner. The doors opened with a soft hiss, revealing an expansive control room that looked like it belonged in a spy thriller—sleek consoles, holographic displays, and walls lined with monitors showing global activities.

"This," Eagle Eye gestured grandly, "is where we monitor everything. Every Shift activity, every governmental move, and more importantly, where we coordinate our efforts to maintain balance."

Maximus stepped forward, examining the technology with an expert eye. "Impressive," he muttered, his gaze lingering on a live feed of a bustling foreign marketplace.

Elizabeth, holding Madison's hand tightly, felt a mix of awe and unease. "And all this, operated under the guise of a bed and breakfast?"

"Exactly," Eagle Eye replied. "Under the radar, hidden in plain sight. The best way to protect our operations from prying eyes."

Christopher, ever the tech enthusiast, was already tapping at a console, his curiosity piqued by the technology at his fingertips. "This system is decades ahead of anything in the public sector," he marveled, looking over at Maximus with excitement brimming in his eyes.

Eagle Eye watched them all, her expression unreadable. "While the technology is impressive, it's merely a tool. Our real strength lies in our people—Shifts like you, who can do extraordinary things. Which brings us to the reason you're all here."

Maximus, who had been quietly observing everything, finally spoke, his voice firm. "You brought us here under the pretense of safety and training, but there's more to it, isn't there?"

Eagle Eye met his gaze squarely. "Yes, there is. The world is changing, Maximus. Shifts are emerging everywhere, and not all have intentions as noble as yours. We need to be prepared to act, not just react. We need a team, and not just any team—an elite unit capable of handling situations that no ordinary human could."

"And you want us," Elizabeth interjected, her protective instincts flaring up as she glanced at Madison. "What exactly are you asking of us? Of her?" She gestured to her daughter, her worry palpable.

Eagle Eye softened slightly, her tone sincere. "I know it's a lot to ask. But Madison, like you, has abilities that could change the course of conflicts before they escalate. We want to train you, guide you, and yes, ask for your help when the time comes."

Maximus nodded slowly, processing the weight of her words. "And if we agree, what then? We just jump into this new life?"

"Not jump," Eagle Eye corrected gently. "Step. Step into your new roles with training, support, and the knowledge that you're not just protecting yourselves, but potentially thousands, if not millions, of others."

The room fell silent, the hum of the technology the only sound. Each person was lost in their own thoughts, the decision before them monumental.

Finally, it was Madison who broke the silence, her young voice steady and surprisingly mature. "I want to help, Mommy. If I can make things better, I want to try."

Elizabeth hugged her daughter tightly, tears brimming in her eyes. "Then we'll do it together."

Maximus stepped forward, extending his hand to Eagle Eye. "We're in. Show us what we need to do."

Eagle Eye clasped his hand, her expression resolute. "Welcome to the Parthenon team. Let's get started."

With that, they turned as a group and walked back into the heart of the facility, ready to begin their new journey, not just as individuals with extraordinary abilities, but as a team with a purpose that stretched far beyond themselves.

# CHAPTER
## THIRTY—FOUR

**M**aximus sat in his office at UCLA, staring at a piece of paper. Everything was unfolding so rapidly, even for him—a man accustomed to unpredictable situations and ready to risk his life at any moment. But now, sitting here, contemplating what lay ahead for them all, even Maximus felt weary.

He would train them well, not only to fight but to think strategically.

A knock on the door jolted him from his thoughts.

"Come in," he called.

Eric and Lily walked in, hesitation etched on their faces. Of course, Eric was the first to speak. "Doc, is it bad?"

"Is what bad?"

"Well, you asked to see us both after class."

"Oh, no, it's nothing like that. Please, come in and have a seat," Maximus reassured them, though he was still uncertain how to broach the subject of his wanting them to join their undercover operation.

The two students entered their professor's office, accustomed to his stern demeanor. "How are you both feeling?" he asked, his expression unreadable.

They exchanged glances.

"Um, I'm feeling okay," Lily offered.

"Yeah, I'm fine," Eric added.

Maximus observed them silently for a moment, the atmosphere growing uncomfortable. "Lily, I noticed you're no longer wearing your two sweaters in the middle of the summer."

Lily chuckled. "That was strange, wasn't it? I just had a persistent cold and couldn't shake it. That was months ago, I'm okay now."

"Eric, I noticed you were absent for a while. Are you feeling better too?" Maximus asked pointedly.

"Yeah, yeah, I'm good. I think I caught Lily's cold."

Maximus's stoic facade remained. "Let's take a walk, shall we?"

They walked down the quad on an unusually warm, sunny day typical for Los Angeles at this time of year.

Birds chirped.

College students tossed a football around. The large campus seemed less safe than Maximus remembered.

"Let me begin by saying that I've always considered the two of you to be my favorite students," he said, catching them off guard.

"Really?" Lily asked, half-jokingly adding, "Eric, too?"

She couldn't resist teasing Eric.

"Hey, well okay..." Maximus chuckled.

The two were used to the professor's humor in class, but here he seemed more approachable, more human. To Lily, Professor Curton was both handsome and dashing—a superstar in her eyes.

"Yes, even Eric. You remind me a lot of myself when I was younger: headstrong, stubborn, not good with authority, and very intelligent. You're just too wrapped up in yourself to show it."

Eric was stunned. "You really think that of me? I always thought you found me irritating, just an annoyance."

"Oh, you are," Maximus quipped. "You are annoying because you have so much potential, but you refuse to use it."

"Professor, something tells me this doesn't have anything to do with class or our grades. What's up?"

"Astute as always," Maximus replied with a grin. "You're right. This has nothing to do with class or grades, but everything to do with your future."

"Doc, I appreciate everything you're saying. Really, I do, but I already told you I'm going to be coaching the pros," Eric proclaimed.

Maximus stopped walking, and Eric and Lily did as well. "So, how are your powers progressing?" Maximus asked suddenly.

Time seemed to freeze; it felt like a bomb had been dropped. Both students were rendered speechless, frozen with shock.

Maximus turned to Lily. "What is it that you can do, Lily?" She looked uncertainly at Eric, unsure how to proceed. Maximus glanced at Eric, "And you?"

Now, Eric looked back at Lily, equally insecure about how to respond. Maximus continued, "Okay, I'll give you a bit more reason to trust me. I too was stricken with the mysterious illness that affected one-third of the world, and I became gravely ill. I awoke three days later, feeling brand new, so to speak."

Eric and Lily were still in shock.

"A short time later, I discovered that I had abilities. Things I couldn't do before. Sound familiar?" Despite his question, neither responded; they simply stared.

"After class one day, I went to grab a book and felt a rush of adrenaline surge through my body, heightening all my senses," Maximus explained.

"So, what can you do?" Eric finally asked, his eyes wide with curiosity.

"I absorbed every word from the book in an instant. I consumed all its knowledge," Maximus revealed.

"Wow," Lily murmured.

"Yeah, that's how I felt. So, I tried it again and the same thing happened. I retained everything from the book I touched."

"Then what?" Eric pressed.

"I didn't know what was happening or what to do. I thought something was wrong," Maximus confessed.

Lily, tears forming, spoke up. "I'm scared, professor. I don't know what to do." Maximus approached her, offering a comforting embrace. "I'm so scared."

"We didn't know what to do or who to tell. We just thought we were freaks. I was afraid the government would come for us, to experiment on us," Eric added, his voice trembling.

Lily stepped back from Maximus, wiping her eyes. "When I figured out what I could do, I went to Eric because I knew he'd been sick too."

"I told her not to tell anyone, not a soul. If we did, our lives could be in danger. So we hid in plain sight," Eric explained.

"We went on with our lives, trying to hide our abilities, but it's not working. The more I try to suppress it, the worse it gets," Lily confessed.

"Exactly," Eric agreed. "I just want it to stop. I just want to be normal again."

"I understand your frustration, and I don't have all the answers yet, but I promise you this: if you come with me, we can find them together," Maximus offered, a resolve settling over him as he prepared them for the uncertain journey ahead.

As the three of them—Maximus, Lily, and Eric—drove along the winding roads of the Santa Monica Mountains, Eric sensed that their lives were about to change irrevocably. Whatever awaited them at their destination, he knew there was no turning back.

Lily hung up her cell phone with a sigh of relief. "Just had to let my mom know I was okay before she went ballistic."

"That's what mothers are for," Maximus remarked, eyes fixed on the road ahead.

Suddenly, a flashing red light erupted on the dashboard, prompting Maximus to veer sharply off the main road. The abrupt turn caught Eric and Lily off guard, sending them lurching in their seats as they scrambled to regain their balance.

"Where are you taking us?" Eric demanded, his voice tense.

"You'll see," Maximus replied, a cryptic smile playing on his lips.

"If we make it there alive!" Lily exclaimed, half-joking, half-serious.

The SUV hurtled towards a cliff. Despite the imminent danger, Maximus showed no signs of slowing down. Panic set in as Eric protested loudly, "Are you going to stop?"

"No," Maximus responded calmly.

"Professor, stop the car!" Lily screamed; terror evident in her voice.

But Maximus remained unfazed, driving them directly towards the cliff's edge. In that heart-stopping moment, as the edge loomed closer, it became clear that Maximus had no intention of stopping.

# CHAPTER
## THIRTY—FIVE

A man clad in a sleek black suit strode purposefully toward the imposing front door of Zaccarie's opulent estate. He delivered a series of rapid, forceful knocks. The door swung open to reveal a butler, his expression as unyielding as stone. "Yes, may I help you?"

"You can tell Zaccarie that Vladimir Egorov is here to settle a debt," the man announced in a thick Russian accent.

"The master is not to be disturbed," the butler responded coolly.

Unsatisfied with this response, Vladimir pushed past the butler and stormed into the grand hallway. "I'm not interested in the Master's preferences. Either you inform him that I'm here, or I will find him myself."

"Very well, sir. Please wait here," the butler conceded, disappearing into the shadowy depths of the corridor.

Vladimir found it surreal to be standing in the house of Zaccarie Lorenz—the man whose near-mythical power was rumored to influence the highest political echelons worldwide. Despite his brother's death eliminating any previous fears of retribution, Zaccarie's promise of no bloodshed had proven false.

Returning with a more pronounced scowl, the butler gestured for Vladimir to follow. "The Master will see you now."

"Finally, he sees sense," Vladimir smirked, shadowing the butler through an intricate maze of corridors until they reached a designated room. "The Master will see you now," the butler repeated, stepping aside.

Vladimir entered the room with such forceful determination that he startled himself. Stories of his temper were legendary, but he hadn't fully believed them until now. Zaccarie stood by a vast window overlooking the gardens, his back to the door.

"Zaccarie, you scum, you lied to me," Vladimir barked as Zaccarie turned slowly, his face breaking into a malevolent grin.

"Vladimir, temper, temper. Hasn't anyone taught you manners? The usual greeting involves a 'hello,'" Zaccarie taunted.

"You dare to lecture me on etiquette when my brother is dead because of your treachery?"

"You'll need to be more specific, Vladimir. Many have died by my hand."

His nonchalant response spurred Vladimir forward, fueling his rage. Zaccarie reveled in the intoxicating waves of anger emanating from him, drawing pleasure from the confrontation as one might savor a fine wine.

"You promised my brother would return safely from that raid, but I learned today he died with the others. You used me!" Vladimir accused.

"My dear Vladimir, I did all within my power to ensure his safety, but the events that transpired were beyond my control," Zaccarie lied smoothly.

"Lies! You wield the power to shape events, Zaccarie! You knew, and yet he died. I will have your throat for this!"

Vladimir, a towering figure at 6'4" and solidly built from years in the family arms trade, approached Zaccarie menacingly. Zaccarie had orchestrated the raid, promising no harm would come to Vladimir's brother, who managed the arms transaction intended to arm a terrorist group. Yet, it ended in a massacre, leaving Vladimir's family devastated and his father mute from grief.

As Vladimir lunged, throwing Zaccarie's antique desk aside as if it were made of straw, his fury only delighted Zaccarie further. Just as Vladimir seized him, ready to exact his revenge, the room shifted unsettlingly beneath his feet.

Looking down in horror, Vladimir saw a liquid-like substance crawling up his legs, immobilizing him. He dropped Zaccarie, who landed with a laugh, reveling in the display of his power.

Unable to move, Vladimir felt the mysterious substance envelop him completely, silencing his threats and turning his rage into fear. Zaccarie watched with sadistic pleasure as Vladimir was transformed into a statue—another addition to his grotesque collection.

A woman emerged from the shadows, her voice tinged with disapproval. "You derive far too much pleasure from this."

"I'm an artist," Zaccarie replied lightly, performing a small, satisfied dance. "Isn't it magnificent?"

"Did the transaction go smoothly?" she asked, knowing the answer but wanting confirmation.

"As if you didn't already know. You're aware of my abilities, as I am of yours," Zaccarie countered, always one step ahead.

"What now?" she pressed.

"We wait," Zaccarie said simply, dismissing her with a wave.

As she turned to leave, Zaccarie's voice stopped her. "There's plenty we could do in the meantime," he suggested, his gaze lingering suggestively.

Despite the chill his words sent down her spine, she approached, touching his face lightly. "For now, Zaccarie, the taste you crave remains but a fantasy," she retorted, withdrawing her hand as if burned.

Zaccarie leaned against his new, chilling artwork, letting her think she had the upper hand—for now. Once he ascended as the supreme ruler, he planned to claim not just her body but her very soul.

# CHAPTER
## THIRTY—SIX

Eric, with his eyes tightly shut, braced for the imminent plunge of the vehicle off the cliff, expecting to hear Lily's screams alongside the crunch of metal impacting the earth. However, none of that happened. Instead, he felt an odd sensation of smooth, uninterrupted motion. Tentatively, he opened his eyes and straightened up in his seat.

To his astonishment, they were still driving. Not only were they not airborne, but they had entered what appeared to be a hidden lair, reminiscent of the Batcave from the Batman comics he used to devour. The corridor they drove through was illuminated with ambient blue lights, guiding their path forward.

Maximus let out a chuckle. "Sorry, kids, I couldn't help myself. The looks on your faces were priceless."

Lily, recovering from her shock and regaining some color, expressed her displeasure. "Professor, why didn't you warn us? I thought we were going to die!" She reached forward and gave him a playful smack on the shoulder from the back seat.

"My apologies," Maximus replied, the car coming to a halt. "I needed you to understand the gravity of the situation. You're about to enter a world from which there is no return."

Eric, his apprehension palpable, voiced his concern. "What if we don't want to be part of this new world?"

"Then I'll turn the car around now, and you'll keep what you've seen to yourselves," Maximus offered with a serious tone.

Lily turned to Eric, her expression earnest. "Eric, what do we have to lose? I'm sick of hiding and not exploring our abilities. Professor Curton is offering us a chance to understand and control what we can do."

After a moment's hesitation, Eric conceded, looking out the window then back at Maximus. "Fine, I'm in."

Maximus smiled warmly. "Thank you for trusting me," he said, as he resumed driving. The car moved deeper into the underground facility, eventually opening into a vast chamber filled with various vehicles. He parked next to a sleek Porsche, drawing a gasp of delight from Eric.

"You like it?" Maximus asked, gesturing towards the Porsche.

"Like it? It's amazing!" Eric exclaimed; his eyes wide.

"It's yours," Maximus stated simply.

Eric paused, stunned. "Seriously?" he asked, skepticism mixing with his excitement.

"As serious as a heart attack," Maximus affirmed.

Eric ran his hand over the hood of the Porsche, his expression one of disbelief. "This is way too cool," he murmured before a thought struck him. "Why? Why give me this?"

"It's the least I can do," Maximus replied, leading them away from the car and towards a set of frosted glass doors.

Lily, still skeptical, echoed Eric's concerns. "Why bring us here just to give us gifts? There's got to be more to this. What's the real reason?"

"If I get caught with this at school, it'll be more trouble than it's worth. What are you playing at, Doc?" Eric added, his tone a mix of paranoia and intrigue.

Maximus led them through the doors into a space that resembled the interior of a spacecraft, causing Eric to marvel aloud at the resemblance. "It's like we're on a spaceship or something."

"That was our reaction, too," Maximus noted as they continued walking.

"Ours?" Lily interjected, her curiosity piqued. "There are others here?"

"Indeed, you are about to meet them, but first, let's make a stop," Maximus replied, pausing before a grand hall that doubled as a hangar bay. "Welcome to Parthenon."

Lily's eyes widened as she took in the expanse of the room, overwhelmed by its scale and the technological marvels it contained. "What is this place?" she exclaimed.

"This is your new home, a sanctuary for Shifts like yourselves," Maximus explained, using the term 'Shifts' to denote those affected by the mysterious phenomenon six months prior.

"Shifts?" Eric repeated, seeking clarification.

Maximus nodded. "That's what we call those of us affected by the event. The world is on the brink of great change. Soon, everyone will know about our abilities. Some will see us as threats; others may seek to exploit us. We need a place where we can learn to control our powers and prepare for what's coming."

"So, you brought us here to train us to fight?" Lily asked, the realization dawning on her.

"Not just to fight," Maximus corrected gently. "To protect ourselves and others from those who might misuse their abilities."

Eric, feeling a newfound sense of purpose, nodded slowly. "I can get behind that."

Lily, still unsure but intrigued by the possibility of no longer having to hide, reluctantly agreed. "Okay, I'm in."

They continued deeper into the facility, where they would meet others like them and begin a new chapter of their lives, one filled with potential and peril.

# CHAPTER
## THIRTY—SEVEN

As Maximus led Eric and Lily through the sprawling corriors of the Parthenon, the sheer scale of the facility continued to impress them. Every corner they turned unveiled new wonders: sprawling labs filled with cutting-edge technology, training rooms equipped with advanced simulations, and communal areas that felt both futuristic and comforting.

They finally arrived at a large, open-plan area bustling with activity. People of all ages were engaged in various tasks—some training, others working on gadgets or discussing animatedly in groups. The energy was palpable, a blend of excitement and serious determination.

"Welcome to the heart of the Parthenon," Maximus announced, his voice filled with a mix of pride and solemnity "This is where we come together, learn from each other, and prepare for whatever challenges lie ahead."

Lily, looking around, felt a surge of nervous excitement. "It's incredible," she whispered, her eyes wide as she took in the scene.

Eric, equally awed but with his typical bravado, chimed in, "Looks like the kind of place where you can really make a difference. Or at least get into some serious trouble."

Maximus chuckled at that, leading them towards a group of individuals who looked up curiously as they approached. "Everyone, I'd like you to meet our newest members, Eric and Lily. They've just joined us today."

The group greeted them warmly, with handshakes and welcoming smiles. Among them was a young woman with striking green eyes, who introduced herself as Ava. "We were all where you are once," she said to Lily and Eric, her voice reassuring. "It's overwhelming at first, but you'll find your place here quickly."

Maximus left them to mingle and pulled aside a man who appeared to be in his late thirties, dressed in a sharp suit but with an approachable demeanor. "Christopher, I need an update on the training modules. How are the new simulations holding up?"

Christopher, who Lily and Eric remembered as Professor Cutty, nodded. "They're ready to go, Maximus. I've incorporated some of the scenarios you suggested, and we've stress-tested them thoroughly. They should give our new recruits a comprehensive grounding in both defensive and offensive strategies."

"That's excellent," Maximus replied, his expression serious. "It's imperative that we get Eric and Lily up to speed as quickly as possible. The sooner they understand their abilities and limitations, the better."

Meanwhile, Eric and Lily were quickly drawn into a discussion about the various aspects of life at the Parthenon. Ava and a few others were explaining the daily routines, which included rigorous physical training, strategy sessions, and, surprisingly, some free time for personal projects and relaxation.

"The balance is important," Ava explained. "We're not just building soldiers here; we're fostering a community. People who can think, act, and react not just as individuals, but as a cohesive unit."

As the day wore on, Eric and Lily participated in their first training session. It was intense and demanding, pushing both of them to the limits of their physical and mental endurance. But it was also exhilarating. For the first time, they were able to openly use their powers, to experiment and learn in a safe environment where their abilities were not only accepted but encouraged.

That night, as they sat in the communal dining area, exhausted but satisfied, Lily turned to Eric. "I never thought I'd say this, but I think we might actually have a chance to do something good here."

Eric, who was usually the more skeptical of the two, couldn't help but agree. "Yeah, it's scary as hell, but it's also kind of amazing. I mean, who gets a chance like this?"

They ate their meal with a newfound sense of camaraderie with their fellow Shifts, all the while knowing that the road ahead would be fraught with challenges. But for now, they were content to be part of something larger than themselves, a place where they could truly belong and make a difference.

# PART 3

## THE BATTLE IS JUST BEGINNING

CHILDREN OF THE SKIES: DESTINY

# CHAPTER
## THIRTY—EIGHT

In a secluded military facility tucked away from prying eyes, a cluster of technicians hunched over a bank of glowing computer monitors. Each wore a badge proclaiming "Homeland Security," their expressions as serious as the classified information they protected. A short, pudgy man with black-rimmed glasses, his shirt meticulously buttoned, rose abruptly from his cluttered desk and hastened toward a dimly lit office at the rear.

Upon entering, he found the room dominated by a single, imposing figure known as Eagle Eye, who sat backlit against the glow of a solitary desk lamp. Her silhouette alone commanded attention.

"We've intercepted something significant from our surveillance bug," he announced, breathless from urgency.

Eagle Eye rose, her presence filling the room with an icy authority. "This had better be worth my time. You and your team have been fumbling around for two weeks with nothing to show," she chastised, her voice cutting through the dim like a knife.

Ignoring her barb, he hurried to a corner of the room and inserted a flash drive into a computer. The wall screen flickered to life, displaying complex genetic sequences. "It appears we've hit jackpot. They've identified a mutation in the DNA, pinpointing exactly where the alteration occurred."

Eagle Eye's eyes gleamed with a mixture of satisfaction and cunning. "Predictable. Maximus always had a knack for uncovering secrets. Why bother with the legwork when he can do it for us?" Her smirk was both triumphant and chilling.

"The team has also tapped into satellite transmissions they've been monitoring. It seems they're zeroing in on the event that triggered these changes," the technician added, scrolling through various feeds.

"And?" Eagle Eye pressed, her patience thinning.

"We're still decrypting the specifics of their findings," he admitted.

"Then make it fast!" she snapped, her command echoing off the stark walls.

As the technician scurried out, Eagle Eye settled back into her chair and resumed a video call on her laptop. "Caught all that?" she queried the image on the screen—Secretary Cortez, a man whose discomfort was palpable even through digital transmission.

"Every word. It sounds like Maximus is on the brink of unraveling the origins of their newfound abilities," Cortez replied, his voice tinged with unease.

"I always said he was a formidable mind," Eagle Eye remarked, her tone laced with a respect that bordered on reverence, yet colored by an underlying strategy that Cortez didn't miss.

"It's time we brought in Theodore Van Spudent, don't you think?" Cortez suggested, shifting uncomfortably.

Eagle Eye paused, her gaze sharp and calculating. "Indeed. Let's see if Mr. Van Spudent can shift the odds in our favor." Her words dripped

with intrigue, hinting at machinations that went far beyond simple surveillance.

This introduction of Mr. Theodore Van Spudent promised a new
layer of complexity to their operations. As Eagle Eye pondered her next
move, the stakes were clearly higher than ever, her chessboard sprawling and dangerous. Her next moves would need to be both precise
and deadly

# CHAPTER
## THIRTY—NINE

In a dimly lit alleyway, members of the notorious Iron Clan, led by the imposing figure of Ares, waited impatiently for Ron's initiation trial to commence. Ron, gripped by anxiety, could only speculate about the nature of the trial as he observed the seasoned members whispering among themselves. Finally, Ares approached with a smirk that did little to ease Ron's nerves.

"Looking a bit jittery there, new blood," Ares taunted.

"Should I be worried?" Ron countered, attempting to mask his apprehension.

"Let's be honest, you're here on Wax's say-so. I personally doubt you've got the mettle for the Iron Clan. Wax thinks otherwise," Ares replied, his voice tinged with skepticism.

Attempting to lighten the mood, Ron joked, "What are you, the bad cop?"

Ares's hands ignited with a vibrant display of red and orange flames, his expression turning serious. "I'm the guy who's about to test if you can handle the heat," he declared ominously.

Just then, an older woman, her appearance reminiscent of a vintage heavy metal icon, joined them. "Are you two done measuring egos, or shall we inform Wax that his new recruit bailed? The truck's almost here."

Ares extinguished his flames and nodded at Ron with a wry smile. "Here's the deal, new blood. An armored truck is about to make a stop at that jewelry store. Usual drill—one guard stays behind, the rest enter with two bags: one black with cash, one silver with diamonds. We grab the black, you get the silver. Prove yourself, and you're in. Understood?"

Ron's heart sank as the reality of the situation dawned on him. He had joined the Clan seeking companionship and a place to belong, but the thought of committing a robbery shook his core. He wasn't a thief, and his powers were meant for more than criminal exploits.

Before Ron could process his thoughts further, the truck turned the corner and parked. The moment of truth had arrived.

As the guards returned from the store, each carrying a bag, Ares strode forward with theatrical confidence. "Excuse me, gentlemen, can I assist you with those bags?" he called out, hands shimmering with an eerie glow.

The guards halted, taken aback by the surreal sight. "What in the world...?" one muttered.

Ares's grin widened as he gestured towards the bags. "I think you'll find we're quite persuasive."

The Clan, lurking in the shadows, chuckled menacingly. Ron, however, felt a profound disconnect. This was not protection; this was provocation.

Ares snapped his fingers, breaking Ron's contemplation. "Time to make your mark, rookie. Grab the silver."

With heavy steps, Ron moved towards his target, his inner conflict raging. As he reached for the bag, a sharp command halted everyone in their tracks.

"Drop your weapons!" the driver shouted, emerging from the truck, pistol shaking in his hand.

Ares scoffed, creating a dramatic spectacle by sending a blast of fire that nudged the truck forward. The guards, overwhelmed by fear, complied, dropping the bags.

As the Clan members moved to collect their spoils, Ron seized the moment. With a surge of adrenaline, he hurled the silver bag at Ares, knocking him off balance.

"Time to rethink our strategies, boys!" Ron yelled, urging the guards into the truck. Just as gunfire erupted, Ron's powers instinctively activated, encasing them in a shimmering golden dome that repelled the bullets.

Inside the truck, Ron urged, "Drive! Now!"

As the vehicle sped away, the dome dissipated, leaving Ares and his crew in a stunned silence, their plan thwarted by the very recruit they had underestimated.

Ron's actions that night not only disrupted the heist but also ignited a spark of rebellion within him. He realized that his powers were not a curse but a potential force for good. As the truck disappeared into the night, Ron contemplated his next move, knowing that his true test had just begun.

# CHAPTER

## FORTY

In a serene meditation chamber surrounded by lush, artificially engineered greenery and a tranquil simulated brook, Maximus, dressed in a flowing white kimono-style robe, presided over a session that seemed more akin to a spiritual retreat than a superhero training camp. Elizabeth, Lily, Madison, and Eric sat on cream-colored yoga mats, their bodies relaxed in the lotus position, each absorbed in the peace that enveloped the room.

A gentle breeze artificially generated yet soothingly real, caressed Elizabeth's skin. She marveled at how her senses had sharpened since the start of her training with Maximus. The wind carried a new essence, a freshness that seemed to whisper secrets directly to her heightened senses. As she focused on her breath, the distinct sensation of energy flowing through the room became palpable—a collective synergy from their unified meditative effort. Suddenly, Madison's thoughts chimed in telepathically, affirming her mother's feelings, a comforting yet startling reminder of her daughter's burgeoning abilities.

Maximus's voice, deep and resonant, broke the silence. "Feel your surroundings. Envision yourself merging with the trees, the grass, and the sky," he instructed, his tone as much a part of the ambiance as the sounds of the flowing water.

As the group delved deeper into their meditative states, personal quirks and fears surfaced subtly among them—Madison's fear of the dark, Lily's peculiar aversion to finishing any drink, and Eric's brashness that often teetered on rudeness.

"Um, sorry, why are we doing this again?" Eric's voice cut through the tranquility, his tone bordering on irritation as he peeked with one eye half-open.

Maximus responded with patient clarity. "Eric, as I've explained, our abilities are intertwined with both the conscious and unconscious mind, and surprisingly, the soul. Yoga and meditation help align these aspects, enhancing our control and strengthening our powers."

"Can't we just go back to fighting? I felt stronger doing that," Eric muttered, clearly unenthused.

"Physical training is just one component, Eric. True mastery comes from aligning the mind, body, and soul. That's when you'll unlock the full potential of your abilities," Maximus explained, his voice firm yet encouraging.

Lily chimed in, supporting the practice, "Some of us actually appreciate this session, Eric. Your negativity is disruptive."

Madison nodded in agreement, "We can all feel it."

Maximus approached Eric, his demeanor calm yet authoritative. "This isn't a game or a sport. This is about survival and being responsible with the powers we possess. You must learn to balance patience with strength."

Reluctantly, Eric resumed his meditation posture, sighing deeply as he closed his eyes once more.

Just then, Christopher's voice interrupted through the comm system. "Maximus, there's a message for you in the control room."

Acknowledging the interruption, Maximus stood and addressed the group, "Continue meditating for another thirty minutes. Elizabeth, you're in charge until I return."

He strode through the simulated forest, disappearing through a portal of shimmering light that whisked him away to the command center. Upon arrival, Christopher awaited with urgent news.

"An encrypted message has come through. Likely from Eagle Eye," Christopher indicated, nodding toward the halo screen.

"Maximus Curton, security clearance Alpha, Tango, Charlie, one-five-seven," Maximus announced, initiating the decryption.

"Security clearance verified. Incoming message decoded," the AI named Tara responded, bringing the screen to life with Eagle Eye's image.

"Maximus, I trust Parthenon is running smoothly. A situation has arisen that fits your project's scope. Ron Etts is currently detained by the Los Angeles police after apparently rescuing guards during an attack by a gang, one of whom wielded pyrokinetic abilities," Eagle Eye briefed with a hint of intrigue in her tone.

Maximus and Christopher exchanged a knowing look, recalling Elizabeth's account of the fiery assailant from the bank heist.

Eagle Eye's message concluded with a directive, "Ron displayed a golden force field during the altercation, safeguarding the guards and facilitating their escape. We've ensured all charges against him will be dropped. I suggest you bring him to Parthenon; he could be a valuable asset. Eagle Eye out."

As the screen faded to black, Christopher quipped, "So, what are we now, babysitters?"

Maximus, sensing the urgency and potential in Eagle Eye's request, replied, "Keep an eye on everything here, Chris. I'll handle this personally."

With a resigned sigh, Christopher muttered, "Babysitters it is."

Maximus swiftly exited, his mind already racing with the possibilities that Ron's unique abilities could bring to their team, and how they might shape the future of Parthenon.

# CHAPTER
## FORTY—ONE

In the stark confines of a Los Angeles police department, Ron Etts delivered his statement with a calm that belied the chaos of his recent life. Normally shackled to a desk beneath the fluorescent glare of corporate life, Ron found the night's events—an entanglement with a gang wielding superpowers and an exchange of gunfire and fireballs—strangely invigorating compared to his daily grind.

As he recounted his tale, Ron noticed the murmurs and sidelong glances from the officers around the station; his story had obviously made the rounds. The detective across from him, a man with a hardened gaze and a trace of disbelief etching his features, finished taking notes and prepared to recap what he'd written.

"Okay, Mr. Etts, just to clarify, I'm going to read this back to you," the detective announced, barely concealing his skepticism. He held the statement with a smirk, as if the words might conjure fiction.

"You already read it back to me," Ron pointed out, his patience waning.

The detective sighed. "On the night of October 28th, you, alongside a group known as the Iron Clan—during what was supposed to be your initiation—allegedly attempted to rob an armored truck. The leader, a man named Mason or 'Ares,' supposedly subdued the guards with pyrokinesis. According to the report, you then defied Ares's orders to kill the guards, turned against him by using a bag of stolen diamonds as a projectile, and somehow generated a golden force field that protected you and the guards from gunfire. All four of you then escaped. Does that sound correct?"

"It sounded right the last several times I recounted it," Ron replied dryly.

"This reads more like a fantasy novel than a police report," the detective muttered, shaking his head. "And yet, four guards are attesting to your heroics. But let me be clear, Mr. Etts, your situation is far from ideal."

As they spoke, an authoritative voice called the detective into the back office labeled 'Chief Ethan Dawson.' The two disappeared behind closed doors, leaving Ron amidst the station's speculative whispers. Moments later, the detective returned, visibly frustrated.

"It seems you've got some influential friends. You're free to go," he announced abruptly.

"I am?" Ron was taken aback.

"Your transportation awaits outside," the detective grumbled, leading Ron to the precinct's front lobby. "If it were up to me, you'd be behind bars. Make sure our paths don't cross again."

Outside, a man approached with a confident stride. "Ron Etts?" he inquired.

"Yes."

"Maximus Curton," he introduced himself, offering a handshake. "Nice to meet you."

Ron shook his hand warily. "How do you know me?"

"The same person who had your charges dropped also happens to be a mutual acquaintance," Maximus explained with a knowing smile.

Ron's bewilderment deepened. "Seems I've made a lot of influential friends lately."

Maximus nodded. "Indeed, and it appears you've found yourself in quite the predicament with the Iron Clan."

"How do you know about that?" Ron interjected, his suspicion piqued.

"Friends in high places," Maximus repeated, a wry edge to his voice.

"I've had my fill of Twilight Zone moments for a while. I was planning on going home to sleep this off for a couple of weeks."

"That would be ill-advised," Maximus cautioned.

"And why's that?" Ron's tone was a mix of exhaustion and defiance.

"Because I have no doubt that your former comrades are keeping tabs on you, and they're not the type to forgive and forget."

A cold dread settled over Ron. "Who's watching my place?"

"Your erstwhile allies from the Iron Clan. They tend to hold grudges."

Ron stood frozen, the reality of his danger dawning on him.

"If you come with me, I can offer you protection and a chance to understand more about your situation," Maximus proposed.

Ron weighed his limited options, the gravity of his predicament anchoring every thought.

"Or you could stay, risk arrest, and an uncertain future in jail," Maximus added, his tone even but firm.

The offer hung in the air, a lifeline amid the swirling chaos of Ron's new reality.

Ron hesitated, weighing the surreal options laid before him. The thought of jail, intertwined with the potential retaliation from the Iron Clan, left a sour taste in his mouth. Maximus's offer, while shrouded in mystery, hinted at a sliver of safety—or at least a path away from immediate danger.

"Alright, I'll go with you," Ron decided, his voice a mix of resignation and curiosity. "But I need some real answers soon."

Maximus nodded, a hint of approval in his gaze. "You'll get them. Let's get out of here."

They walked to a sleek, unmarked vehicle parked discreetly by the curb. As they drove away, the city's lights blurred past, casting elongated shadows that flickered like the remnants of Ron's former life.

The car ride was silent at first, with Ron lost in thought and Maximus respecting his need to process the evening's chaos. After a while, Maximus spoke up.

"We're headed to a facility known as Parthenon," he began, his voice steady. "It's a safe haven for people like you, those who've found themselves with... extraordinary abilities."

Ron looked out the window, the reality of his situation settling in. "Extraordinary abilities... Is that what we're calling it now?"

"In a manner of speaking, yes," Maximus replied. "What happened tonight—the force field you created—that was no fluke. It's a manifestation of something much deeper, something intrinsic to who you are now."

The concept seemed fantastical to Ron, yet undeniably real given the events he had just survived. "And these other people at Parthenon, they're like me?"

"Each with unique abilities, yes. You'll meet others who have been through their own trials, some even more turbulent than yours. You're not alone in this."

As the conversation unfolded, the tension in Ron's shoulders eased slightly. The idea of meeting others who could understand his new reality was a small comfort.

Maximus continued, "At Parthenon, we aim to understand these abilities, harness them for good. But more importantly, we provide a community—a place where you don't have to hide or fear what you've become."

Ron mulled over the words. A part of him yearned for his mundane, predictable life before all this, but another part was intrigued by the prospect of understanding and controlling his newfound power.

"So, what happens next?" Ron asked, his curiosity piqued despite the uncertainty.

"We train, we learn, and we prepare," Maximus answered. "Because the truth is, the world isn't quite ready to accept people like us. And until it is, we need to be ready for whatever comes our way."

Ron nodded, a mix of apprehension and a newfound resolve brewing within him. As the car sped towards its destination, the night's earlier terror transformed into a cautious hope. Perhaps at Parthenon, he could find the answers he desperately needed and a new purpose in this strange, new chapter of his life.

MAXIMUS'S WORDS WERE A MIX OF REASSURANCE AND CHALLENGE, tinged with a hint of mystery that Ron wasn't sure he liked. As the vehicle surged forward, Ron's grip tightened on the dashboard.

"Just trust me," Maximus added, his eyes fixed on the road ahead, which ended abruptly at the cliff's edge.

Ron swallowed hard, his mind racing with thoughts of the newfound abilities he barely understood, let alone controlled. The car sped towards the cliff, and Ron braced for impact or... something unimaginable.

"Ready?" Maximus asked, a smirk playing on his lips.

"Ready for what?" Ron managed to choke out, his voice a mix of fear and intrigue.

Just as the car was about to fly off the cliff, Maximus tapped a concealed button on the dashboard. Suddenly, the vehicle transformed. Panels shifted, and the whole structure shuddered and morphed into a sleek, jet-like form. Thrusters ignited, and instead of plummeting down the mountainside, they soared upward into the sky.

Ron's stomach dropped as they ascended rapidly. He looked over at Maximus, who seemed entirely at ease, if not amused, by Ron's reaction.

"This—this is insane!" Ron exclaimed, his initial shock giving way to a rush of adrenaline.

"It's necessary," Maximus replied, his eyes still on the horizon. "Our abilities come with responsibilities, and sometimes, they require us to push beyond the ordinary limits of human experience."

As they stabilized in the air, Ron took a deep breath, trying to process the reality of flying in a car—or whatever this vehicle had become. The metaphor wasn't lost on him; his life had transformed just as radically and unexpectedly.

"You see, Ron, the world we live in—the world we're preparing you for—it doesn't play by the usual rules," Maximus continued. "And neither do we. At Parthenon, you'll learn not just to control your powers, but to embrace them. To transform fear into something... powerful."

Ron looked out at the expanse of sky before them, feeling a mixture of dread and excitement. This was more than just about surviving or fighting; it was about transcending who he once was.

"And what about the others?" Ron asked, curiosity peaking. "The ones who can't control their powers or use them for harm?"

"That's part of why we need you," Maximus said, turning to face him. "Every team needs members who can bring them back from the edge, who can remind them of who they are and what they fight for. You've got a knack for that, even if you don't know it yet."

Ron pondered this new role, feeling a weight of responsibility suddenly thrust upon him. Yet, there was also a sense of belonging, of being part of something larger than himself, something noble.

As they flew towards Parthenon, the sun dipped below the horizon, casting a golden glow that seemed to herald new beginnings. Ron felt it—a spark of hope, a surge of purpose. Maybe, just maybe, he could be more than what he had been, maybe he could make a difference.

Maximus's voice pulled him from his thoughts, "Welcome to your new life, Ron. Let's make it count."

Ron nodded, his resolve firming. "Let's," he said, facing the horizon and the myriad possibilities that lay beyond.

# CHAPTER
## FORTY—TWO

In a dimly lit room filled with the scent of old books and lingering power, five men gathered around an antique English walnut table, each dressed in meticulously tailored suits that spoke of wealth and silent threats. On the left side of the table sat Davino Ricci and Luca Costa, men of keen intellect and cold calculation. Opposite them were Luigi Conti and Riccardo De Luca, each a master of their own domain within the clandestine world of Cosa Nostra. At the head of the table, commanding respect through both presence and reputation, was Zano Bianchi, the venerable elder statesman rarely seen but universally respected.

Bianchi, despite his reclusive nature due to age and declining health, had convened this meeting of the five families to address the tumultuous ascension of Zaccarie and his troubling illness—facts that Zaccarie believed were concealed, yet were as transparent as glass in the world these men operated in.

The heavy door creaked open, heralding Zaccarie's entrance. His step was confident, his smile a mask of arrogance poorly disguising the entitlement born from a vast inheritance and a legacy more feared than revered.

Zaccarie, settling into the seat directly across from Bianchi, greeted them with a veneer of cordiality, "Buona sera, colleghi. As my Italian is somewhat rusty, may we proceed in English to spare the beautiful language from my less practiced tongue?"

Zeno Bianchi, his voice heavy with Sicilian inflections, acknowledged him coolly. "That, among other reasons, is why we are gathered, Zaccarie."

"Oh? I'm intrigued. What seems to be the concern?" Zaccarie responded with feigned ignorance.

Luigi Conti was quick to cut through the pretense. "It's about adherence to the sacred laws of our order, which you, Zaccarie, have flaunted rather than respected."

Davino Ricci added, "The law mandates that any leader showing signs of sickness must step down. Yet here you sit, questioning tradition."

Zaccarie's eyes narrowed. "Do I appear unwell to you all? Am I not the very image of health?"

"Your insolence knows no bounds," Riccardo De Luca spat, his patience thinning.

Zeno raised a hand, signaling for calm. "We are aware of your condition, Zaccarie. It is time for you to step aside."

"I shall do no such thing," Zaccarie retorted with a scoff. "Your traditions are relics, as obsolete as this council."

"The price of defiance is steep," Zeno warned, his voice a low growl.

Zaccarie leaned back, his gaze calculating as he assessed Zeno, the linchpin in his tenuous hold over the families. "I remember being terrified of clowns as a child," he began, an odd smirk playing on his lips.

"It's the fear... that icy dread that creeps up your spine, much like the fear you instill in your enemies before their demise."

Silence enveloped the room, heavy and thick. The air grew tense, charged with an unspoken understanding of the threat looming in Zaccarie's words.

Zeno's face paled as he felt an unnatural cold seep into his legs. Glancing down in horror, he saw his chair dissolve into a viscous, creeping sludge that climbed his body relentlessly.

"There's the look," Zaccarie murmured as he watched the fear morph into horror on Zeno's face. Within moments, the elder was encapsulated, a permanent fixture in Zaccarie's twisted gallery.

"You questioned my vitality and my power," Zaccarie continued, his voice cold as the grave. "Consider this a demonstration of both. Are we all in agreement now?"

The men, once lords of their realms, sat frozen, their voices stolen by the spectacle before them. Zaccarie stood, his departure as smooth and unruffled as if he had merely chaired a mundane business meeting.

"Meeting adjourned," he declared nonchalantly, his footsteps echoing off the stone as he left the room, leaving behind a silence that spoke volumes of the new era dawning—one ruled by fear, not respect.

# CHAPTER
## FORTY—THREE

Christopher and Maximus stood in the control room, with Ron wedged between them, absorbing the gravity of the situation. The details had been laid out exhaustively, and Ron, appearing overwhelmed, blinked as if caught in a spotlight.

"You're recruiting me into your club?" Ron asked, a hint of incredulity lacing his words.

"More or less," Maximus admitted with a nonchalant shrug.

"I just escaped from those maniacs..." Ron's frustration was palpable, his distrust evident.

"We're not criminals," Christopher chimed in, attempting to offer some reassurance.

"Says who? From a certain perspective, you might seem just as suspect," Ron countered, his skepticism undimmed.

"We aim to prevent harm, not incite wars like your former acquaintances in the Iron Clan," Maximus clarified, trying to draw a clear distinction.

Ron sighed, the weight of his experiences pressing down upon him. "I don't know what to think anymore," he confessed, feeling utterly lost.

"Listen to that still, small voice in the back of your mind. What's it telling you?" Maximus encouraged gently, sensing Ron's internal struggle.

After a moment of contemplation, Ron admitted, "That I'm safe here, and I can trust you."

"There you have it," Christopher exclaimed, a broad smile breaking across his face as if they had crossed a major hurdle.

"Let's go meet some folks you ought to know," Maximus suggested, leading the way out of the command center. They hadn't walked far when they encountered Elizabeth, wiping sweat from her brow and clutching a water bottle.

"Elizabeth," Maximus greeted her cordially.

"Maximus, welcome back. And who's this?" Elizabeth's curiosity piqued as she eyed Ron.

"This is Ron. He's going to be staying with us," Maximus introduced him, his tone warm.

"It's nice to meet you, Ron," Elizabeth extended a hand, her welcoming smile genuine.

"Where are the others?" Maximus inquired, looking around.

"They're in the simulation room, sparring," Elizabeth informed, taking a sip of her water.

"Eric and Lily are sparring with Madison?" Maximus raised an eyebrow, concern tinting his voice.

"Don't worry, Madison can hold her own," Elizabeth reassured him with a chuckle.

"I have no doubt. But just to be sure, we'll go take a look," Maximus decided, leading Ron down the hallway.

"I'm off to see Chris. I'll join you guys at seven for meditation," Elizabeth said as she departed.

"Meditation?" Ron echoed, intrigued.

Maximus explained, "Through meditation, we can harness and enhance our powers. It's quite transformative. You'll see."

Arriving at a set of shaded glass doors, Maximus gestured casually and a miniature halo screen appeared. With a few swift taps, he deactivated the camouflage.

Beyond the doors lay not just a room, but a sprawling desert landscape. Ron gaped in astonishment as he watched three figures demonstrate remarkable abilities: tangible energy waves, freezing objects, and telekinesis.

"Welcome to the simulation room. We can simulate any environment here. It seems they chose a desert today," Maximus remarked casually.

He entered the command to open the doors, and the heat from the simulated desert washed over them.

"Program, freeze," Maximus commanded, and instantly, the environment paused, though the individuals remained animated.

Madison ran up to them, her eyes sparkling with excitement. "Did you see? I lifted a boulder! The meditation's really helping!" She then noticed Ron, her expression shifting to curiosity. "Who's this?"

Maximus introduced Ron to Madison, and then to Eric and Lily as they approached. Eric, sizing Ron up with a critical eye, merely nodded in acknowledgment.

"You'll have to excuse Eric; subtlety isn't his strong suit," Lily joked, extending her hand warmly to Ron.

Maximus cleared his throat, "Now that introductions are out of the way, it's time."

"Time for what?" Ron asked, one eyebrow arched in question.

"To train," Maximus declared with a knowing smile.

"Wait," Madison interrupted eagerly, "Lily, we have to tell Maximus about the new names we've come up with!"

Maximus looked puzzled. "Names?"

"Yeah, Madison thought it'd be cool since we're like, in hiding and have these secret powers, to have code names!" Lily explained with a grin.

Maximus considered this, then smiled at Ron. "Maybe that's a discussion for another time. Let's give Ron a chance to settle in first."

"Okay," Madison agreed, slightly deflated but understanding.

As they exited the simulation room, the group felt a renewed sense of camaraderie and purpose. Maximus knew the integration of Ron into their unique family was just beginning, but he was confident in the path forward. They weren't just a team; they were a burgeoning force for change.

# CHAPTER
## FORTY—FOUR

Frank Sirs had been a security guard at the news station for more years than he cared to count. His mornings were a well-worn routine: a stop at the local coffee shop for a black coffee with two sugars, followed by a quick visit to the corner newsstand for the day's newspaper. Then he'd head to work, clock in, and settle behind his desk to sign in visitors.

He generally enjoyed his job.

The occasional disturbance broke the monotony, but nothing ever happened that he and the other security guards couldn't handle. Yet today felt different; he was unusually irritable. Perhaps it was the anticipation of his upcoming vacation—a long-awaited Hawaiian getaway with his wife, something she had dreamed of for years. Despite the financial strain, he believed she was worth every penny. His thoughts were interrupted by a flicker on one of the mini surveillance screens. Something had moved past camera six in the elevator shaft.

Curious, Frank leaned closer to the screen just as the anomaly reappeared.

He reached for the walkie-talkie. "Hey Shirley, are there any maintenance crews in the shafts today?"

A crackle of static preceded her response. "Not that I'm aware of, Sirs. What's up?"

"Thought I saw something. I'm going to check it out."

"Want backup?"

"Nah, probably just a rat or something," Frank dismissed the need for concern.

"Alright, keep me posted."

Frank left his desk and headed toward the maintenance room. The door creaked open, releasing a wave of musty, sour air. He hated going down there—it always reminded him of those old horror films where nightmares lurked around every corner. He checked camera six; it seemed to be functioning correctly. After a thorough scan of the area revealed nothing unusual, he radioed back.

"Shirley, looks clear here. Camera's fine, but—"

His words were cut off abruptly. Silence followed, then a static burst over the walkie-talkie.

"Frank? Frank, come in!" Shirley's voice grew anxious.

There was no reply. In the dim light of the maintenance room, only Frank's walkie-talkie lay on the ground, his sudden disappearance marking the beginning of an unforeseen mystery.

SEVERAL MEN STRODE INTO THE STATION, THEIR LEADER, JOSE Martinez, at the forefront. "Do you have everything ready?" he inquired of the man beside him, who clutched a briefcase.

"All set," the man confirmed.

They boarded the elevator, ascending to the top floor. As the elevator doors slid open, they were greeted by the hustle and bustle of a busy studio. Instantly, the atmosphere shifted as the thugs, brandishing semi-automatic weapons, stepped out. One of them fired rounds into the air, shattering the mundane tranquility.

"Please, forgive my friend's impatience," Jose, now known as Wax, declared with a sardonic calm. "But it was important to get your attention."

The other men swiftly dispersed throughout the room, securing the area. The two anchors at the desk paled, their faces draining of color as the reality of the situation dawned on them. Wax approached the desk, his demeanor cool and commanding. "If you don't mind, I need to speak to the American people. I would rather do it alone."

The anchors scrambled from their seats, leaving them spinning in their haste. One of the men stowed his weapon and took position behind the camera, while another commandeered the control room, preparing to broadcast Jose's message. Employees lay on the ground, immobilized by fear, as the makeshift crew got ready. The cameraman silently counted down with his fingers: three, two, one. A red light flickered on, signaling they were live.

"Greetings, ladies and gentlemen," Wax began, his voice resonating with newfound authority. "My name is Wax, and I have an important message for you all." Now recognized as the leader of the Iron Clan, the destruction and chaos his gang had wrought throughout the city had reshaped his identity. No longer the abandoned boy yearning for approval and affection, Jose Martinez reveled in his command and the fear he instilled. As Wax, he was not just a survivor but a ruler of his destiny, savoring the direction it was taking.

Wax's gaze locked onto the camera, his expression steely and unwavering. "Tonight, we take a stand not just for ourselves, but for every forgotten soul who's ever felt powerless. Today, we harness that power for a cause."

He paced slightly, the camera following his movements, capturing the intensity that emanated from him. "The authorities label us criminals, renegades, outcasts. But today, we reveal the truth. We are the awakened ones, and our actions will pave the way for a new order."

Behind him, the room remained eerily silent, the crew and hostages alike caught in the gravity of his address. Wax continued, his voice a mix of venom and charisma. "We will no longer be silent. We will no longer be invisible. Our powers, our very existence, threaten those who cling to the old ways because we embody change."

He leaned in closer to the camera, his eyes burning with fervor. "This is not an act of terrorism, but a declaration of our emergence. To those who wield power without Alexandra, who enforce law without compassion, we are your reckoning."

Turning to address someone off-camera, Wax signaled to cut the feed. The screen went black, leaving viewers worldwide in stunned silence, grappling with the implications of his message.

As the broadcast ended, Wax turned to his crew, his face shifting from the public mask of defiance to a more contemplative expression. "Ensure everyone here is unharmed but secure. We leave in ten minutes; our message is delivered, but our work has just begun."

Outside the studio, the sound of sirens began to swell as law enforcement converged on the location. Wax's calm demeanor belied the urgency of their situation, but he was prepared. This broadcast was just the first move in a much larger strategy.

Back in the command center, Maximus watched the unfolding scene on multiple screens, his brow furrowed. "Christopher, gather everyone. It's time we discuss our response. Wax's actions tonight will escalate tensions between Shifts and the government, and we must be ready."

Christopher nodded, tapping commands into a console. "I'll inform the others. This is going to change everything, isn't it?"

Maximus turned away from the screens, his mind racing with potential scenarios. "Yes, it will. And we need to be prepared for every single one of them. It's not just about protecting ourselves now—it's about defining what we stand for."

As the team convened, the weight of their responsibility hung heavy in the air. They were not just defending their own; they were shaping the future of all who had been changed.

# CHAPTER
## FORTY—FIVE

Christopher lounged in the control room, tucked beneath the console with the halo screen displaying morning cartoons—a ritualistic relapse into his childhood delights. His laughter mingled with the antics of Wile E. Coyote and the Roadrunner until an abrupt switch interrupted his amusement. The screen flickered to Wax's broadcast, compelling Christopher to emerge with urgency and crank up the volume.

Wax's voice filled the room. "There is a grave secret that the governments of the world are keeping from you, one that will change the course of human history forever. Those of us who fell ill almost a year ago have since transformed, becoming something else entirely...."

Captivated and alarmed, Christopher dashed to the intercom. "Everyone, I'm streaming a feed from the station I'm watching," he announced, ensuring all in Parthenon could bear witness.

Screens lit up across the facility—kitchen, simulation room, and elsewhere—as Maximus rushed into the command center, his face etched with concern.

Wax continued, his tone escalating. "We have unearthed abilities—abilities beyond reason and comprehension. Abilities that we are now poised to demonstrate. Long live the Iron Clan!"

Christopher turned to Maximus, the weight of the moment settling between them. "What does this mean?" he asked.

Maximus's expression was grave. "I fear this marks the beginning of an upheaval."

The broadcast cut to a dramatic scene set against the Hollywood hills. A man with fiery red hair, his hands aglow with pulsing red and orange energy, unleashed a burst of fire into the dry brush, igniting it instantly. The cameras captured the ensuing chaos, the shrill screams piercing through the broadcast.

As the team gathered, the horror unfolded further; the camera panned to a man whose physical form expanded monstrously, lifting a car and hurling it effortlessly.

The feed went dark, plunging the room into a stunned silence, broken only by the heavy breaths of the team.

"This," Maximus declared, turning to address his team, "is why we train. To stop those who misuse their powers from wreaking havoc. We are going to intervene."

Eric bounced eagerly. "That's what I'm talking about!"

"Plan of action," Maximus instructed swiftly, "Eric, Lily, and I will survey from the helicopter. Elizabeth and Ron, you're on ground support in an all-terrain vehicle. Chris, Madison, you stay here. We need eyes and ears on the ground."

Madison pouted, moving toward Maximus. "Why can't I fight too?"

Maximus knelt to her level, a gentle firmness in his voice. "I need you here, Madison. You and Chris are vital to our coordination."

Her disappointment gave way to resolve, a smile breaking across her face.

"Everyone, remember your training. Watch each other's backs," Maximus rallied as they dispersed to their assignments.

At the hangar, the team moved with precision. Maximus, Lily, and Eric boarded the high-tech helicopter, the anticipation palpable. Maximus slipped into the pilot's seat, his fingers dancing over the controls.

Tara's voice chimed in, crisp and clear. "Good morning, Maximus."

"Morning, Tara. Start her up. Let's see what she's got," he commanded.

The hangar doors retracted, revealing the open sky. As the helicopter lifted off, the thrill of the ascent coursed through them—Lily's excited screams mingling with the roar of rotors.

Maximus's gaze was steely, focused. Despite the adrenaline, a part of him pondered the rustiness of his own instincts. As the helicopter ascended rapidly, he pressed a button, his voice carrying over the cabin's hum.

"Strap in."

The helicopter soared upward, its blades slicing through the clouds, its passengers bound together by a shared mission and an uncertain future.

# CHAPTER
## FORTY—SIX

In a scene ripped from nightmares, the local populace fled in terror as fire rampaged through the foothills, devouring home after home in a relentless inferno. Above the chaos, from the relative safety of the high-tech helicopter, Ares's maniacal laughter resonated, his enjoyment of the terror below palpable and disturbing.

The helicopter, dubbed Pegasus, arrived on the scene first. From her seat, Lily scanned the ground, her voice tense with urgency. "Is that someone down there, in the middle of all this?"

Maximus, piloting the helicopter, followed her gaze, his expression grim. "It seems he's the instigator."

As they hovered closer, the figure on the ground—his identity hidden by the flames and smoke—turned his attention towards them. A wave of fiery energy surged upwards, narrowly missing Pegasus.

Maximus maneuvered the helicopter expertly, a wry smile crossing his face despite the danger. "It's heating up in here," he remarked dryly.

Lily, ever the combatant, responded with a smirk. "Land this bird, and I'll give him a taste of a real cooldown."

Their banter did little to mask the gravity of their mission as they prepared to confront the chaos below, ready to intervene and halt the destruction.

As Ron and Elizabeth approached the city, the extent of the chaos became painfully apparent. Cars were haphazardly tossed aside, buildings bore the scars of damage, and the air was filled with the screams of people, a stark contrast to the surrounding destruction.

"It looks like we can't go any further in the truck. We'll have to continue on foot," Elizabeth observed.

"Chris, can you hear us?" Ron asked, tapping the communication device.

"Loud and clear," Christopher's voice echoed through their earpieces, sounding both omnipresent and distant.

"Can you pinpoint where they've headed?" Ron continued, scanning the horizon for any sign of the perpetrators.

"Give me a second to bounce a signal off a satellite... I'll find out whether they're hiding or literally tearing up the town," Christopher quipped.

Ron exchanged a glance with Elizabeth, who smirked slightly. "Chris is an acquired taste," she whispered.

After a moment, Christopher's voice returned, more serious this time. "They're about a quarter mile north from your current position. The big one is literally ripping the city apart, and the others aren't far behind, causing havoc. Be careful..."

"Thanks, Chris," Ron responded swiftly, his tone tinged with urgency. They climbed out of the truck, prepared for the grim task ahead as they moved towards the heart of the destruction.

MAXIMUS FOUND A SECURE LOCATION TO LAND THE HIGH-TECH helicopter, Pegasus, amidst the rapidly spreading inferno that threatened to consume the entire city.

"Head out and contain the fire while I take on the arsonist," Maximus commanded.

"That's reckless—he'll incinerate you! Eric and you manage the fire, and I'll handle our fiery adversary," Lily countered firmly.

"Her point stands, Doc," Eric supported, nodding.

After a brief moment of reflection, Maximus acknowledged the validity of her argument. "Fine, but be cautious and remain sharp," he cautioned Lily.

"Understood. Now go!" she insisted.

The two men dashed towards the urban center.

Lily momentarily watched them blend into the smoky haze before focusing on the daunting challenge ahead. Gathering her resolve, she advanced towards Ares, parting the flames with surges of icy energy.

Ares reveled in uproarious laughter. "Really? They send a mere girl to confront a god?" he scoffed upon noticing her.

As Lily approached Ares, the heat grew unbearable, as if she were in the core of the sun. Summoning her abilities, she wrapped herself in a radiant shield of icy light.

"That shield won't protect you," he sneered, hurling a volley of fire towards her.

Nimbly, Lily evaded his attacks, responding with sharp blasts of cold.

Ares, nimble himself, dodged her counterattacks, firing back with increased ferocity.

Once again, Lily raised her hand, releasing a potent wave of cold. This time, it encased a nearby tree.

The intense heat clashed with the ice, shattering it into a myriad of pieces.

"Quite cunning, little girl," Ares taunted, preparing another fiery onslaught.

Their clash continued unabated, a vivid display of opposing forces, as light dueled with darkness, and fire clashed with ice.

THE FIRE HAD REACHED A HOUSE, TRAPPING A FAMILY OF THREE inside. The mother's screams echoed as she urged her husband to escape with their daughter, but the advancing flames threatened to engulf them all. Maximus and Eric, witnessing the dire situation, rushed toward the burning home.

Maximus plunged into the house without hesitation. "Eric, stop the fire!" he called back over his shoulder.

"How?" Eric yelled, bewildered.

"Use sound waves!" Maximus's voice was almost drowned out by the roar of the fire.

Hearing the woman's screams intensify, Eric glanced up to see the flames licking the front door. He lifted his hand and projected high-powered acoustical sound waves directly at the fire.

To his astonishment, the flames began to recede.

Moments later, Maximus emerged, guiding the man, woman, and their infant to safety.

"How did you know that would work?" Eric asked, still stunned.

"The waves create a drop in air pressure, starving the fire of oxygen," Maximus explained.

"Oh," Eric muttered.

"Perhaps you should have paid more attention in physics," Maximus remarked with a half-smile, relieved yet focused on the crisis at hand.

ELIZABETH AND RON CONVERGED ON WAX AND HIS MEN AS CHAOS erupted around them. A shootout with the police was in full swing, with Wax violently dismantling an armored police vehicle, hurling officers through the air as if they were mere dolls.

In an instant, Elizabeth sprinted up a mound of discarded cars and launched herself into the sky, her foot connecting with an armed thug's chest. The policemen stopped firing, struck by a moment of sheer astonishment. Tucking into a roll, she sprung back into the air and executed a perfect spin kick, knocking down three more assailants in a swift, fluid motion.

The Clan, seeing her formidable skills, opened fire. Elizabeth darted like a gust of wind, seeking refuge alongside the police officers. "Hey boys, having fun yet?" she quipped, catching her breath.

Meanwhile, Ron faced Wax directly.

"Yo, big guy, ever fight someone your own size?" Ron taunted.

Wax paused, visibly irked by the challenge. With a grunt, he hurled the armored vehicle toward Ron. Without hesitation, Ron extended his hand, halting the vehicle mid-air. With a forceful thrust, he sent it flying back at Wax, toppling the brute to the ground. Cheers erupted from the police as their formidable adversary lay dazed on the pavement.

STREAMS OF BLUE AND RED LIGHT PAINTED THE SKY AS A FIERCE battle raged within the fire. Ares, growing impatient with the standoff, unleashed a scorching onslaught of fire waves toward Lily.

She responded with determined vigor, her hands dispatching icy blasts to counter the heat. Despite her efforts, Ares intensified his attack, his body radiating heat so intense it scorched the earth around him. Lily felt her strength wane, and a fleeting thought crossed her mind—this might be her end. Guilt from her past actions weighed heavily on her, convincing her she deserved this fate.

But then, a voice resonated within her, clear and unwavering—it was Madison.

"Lily, don't give up. Remember your training," Madison's voice echoed in her mind. "Remember what Maximus taught us. Don't succumb to fear. Focus your mind, body, and soul as one, and nothing can defeat you."

Madison's voice faded as swiftly as it had appeared, leaving Lily with a renewed sense of purpose. She closed her eyes, envisioning herself in the simulation room, serene and composed in the lotus position, the cool air soothing her face. When she reopened her eyes, she radiated a brilliant aura of ambient blue light.

With newfound control, she deflected Ares's next wave of fire and soared into the sky, landing gracefully on a newly formed sheet of ice. She continued, creating a cascading staircase of ice, ascending towards the heavens.

Lily executed a flawless flip to land behind Ares.

"Freeze," she commanded, unleashing a mighty torrent of cold energy.

The chill enveloped Ares, trapping him within an icy prison. She approached him; he was immobilized but alive, sidelined for the moment.

Turning her attention to the rampant fire, Lily bent down, her hand touching the scorched earth. "Focus," she whispered to herself.

She exhaled slowly, and a gentle light flowed from her hands, spreading through the surrounding area. The inferno yielded to her calming influence, receding as speckles of blue light emerged from Lily and danced through the air. Soon, the once-threatening flames had vanished, leaving a delicate frost in their wake.

Lily smiled to herself. If she hadn't joined Maximus those months ago, none of this would have been possible. As she hurried to reunite with her comrades, she knew without a doubt that she had made the right decision.

IN THE CHAOTIC AFTERMATH OF DESTRUCTION, WAX STRUGGLED to his feet, his resolve doubled. With a wild look in his eyes, he charged toward Ron, bulldozing through obstacles as he aimed to confront the man who had betrayed him. As Wax neared, Ron calmly raised his hands and unleashed a powerful energy wave, lifting Wax off his feet and crashing him through a retaining wall.

While Wax was temporarily incapacitated, Ron seized the opportunity. With a deft motion, he halted the bullets fired by Wax's cohorts, then, with a flick of his wrist, he sent another wave that melted the guns in their hands.

Amidst the gunfire, one of Wax's men—the same man Ron had saved on the beach days earlier—prepared his own counterattack. He tilted his head back, opened his mouth, and unleashed a torrential gust of wind. Cars, debris, and people were swept up as if caught in a tempest.

Elizabeth, gripping a protruding metal rod, managed to catch a policeman just before he was sucked into the maelstrom. Nearby, Ron conjured an energy shield, enveloping several officers, shielding them from the chaos as he searched for a clear shot at their assailant.

Just as the wind ceased, Wax attempted to rise, only to be met with a sonic wave from an unseen source that slammed him against a building with a resonant thud.

As the airborne debris settled back to the earth, Elizabeth and Ron noticed Eric, Maximus, and Lily regrouping nearby, their surroundings a battlefield of uprooted fire hydrants and cascading water, giving the illusion of rain.

The officers stood dumbfounded, still processing the swift turn of events. Wax, meanwhile, seemed poised to flee.

"Enough!" Maximus bellowed. "It's over."

"It will never be over," Wax retorted defiantly, his voice booming through the turmoil. "The Iron Clan lives!" With that, he hurled himself toward a building.

"NO!" Maximus roared in response.

Eric, quick to react, unleashed a barrage of sonic emissions that halted Wax's escape. Despite Wax's attempts to advance, Eric's relentless assault eventually brought him to his knees.

However, the structural damage to the surrounding buildings was already taking its toll. The skyscraper nearby began to sway ominously, a tremor crawling up its frame as windows shattered, showering the streets below with glass.

Lily sprinted toward the group, forming a protective ice shield overhead to guard against the falling debris. Simultaneously, Eric converted the descending glass into harmless dust with another wave of his energy.

In that critical moment, as all seemed lost with the skyscraper teetering dangerously, something extraordinary occurred. The environment shifted; the air grew dense, and the cascading water froze mid-fall.

Maximus, bewildered, scanned the surreal scene. The halted building and the suspended figures in mid-air were inexplicable.

Then, he heard Lily's urgent call. "Maximus, look..."

His gaze followed hers to an astonishing sight: Ron, suspended above the ground, his eyes ablaze with a fierce silver light.

Ron, seemingly the orchestrator of this miraculous stasis, raised his hand, and the fragmented building and its occupants gently ascended, reassembling seamlessly as if guided by an unseen architect. The damage reversed, the fissure sealing as if it had never existed.

With a sweeping gesture, Ron directed a beam of ambient light at Wax and the other remaining members of the Iron Clan, who vanished in an instant. He then targeted Ares with a decisive motion, and as he did, the suspended water resumed its fall, returning to normalcy as if time itself had been reset.

As Ron's eyes dimmed and he collapsed, exhausted from his exertions, those around him remained in stunned silence, their awe shared by the world that had witnessed this display of power.

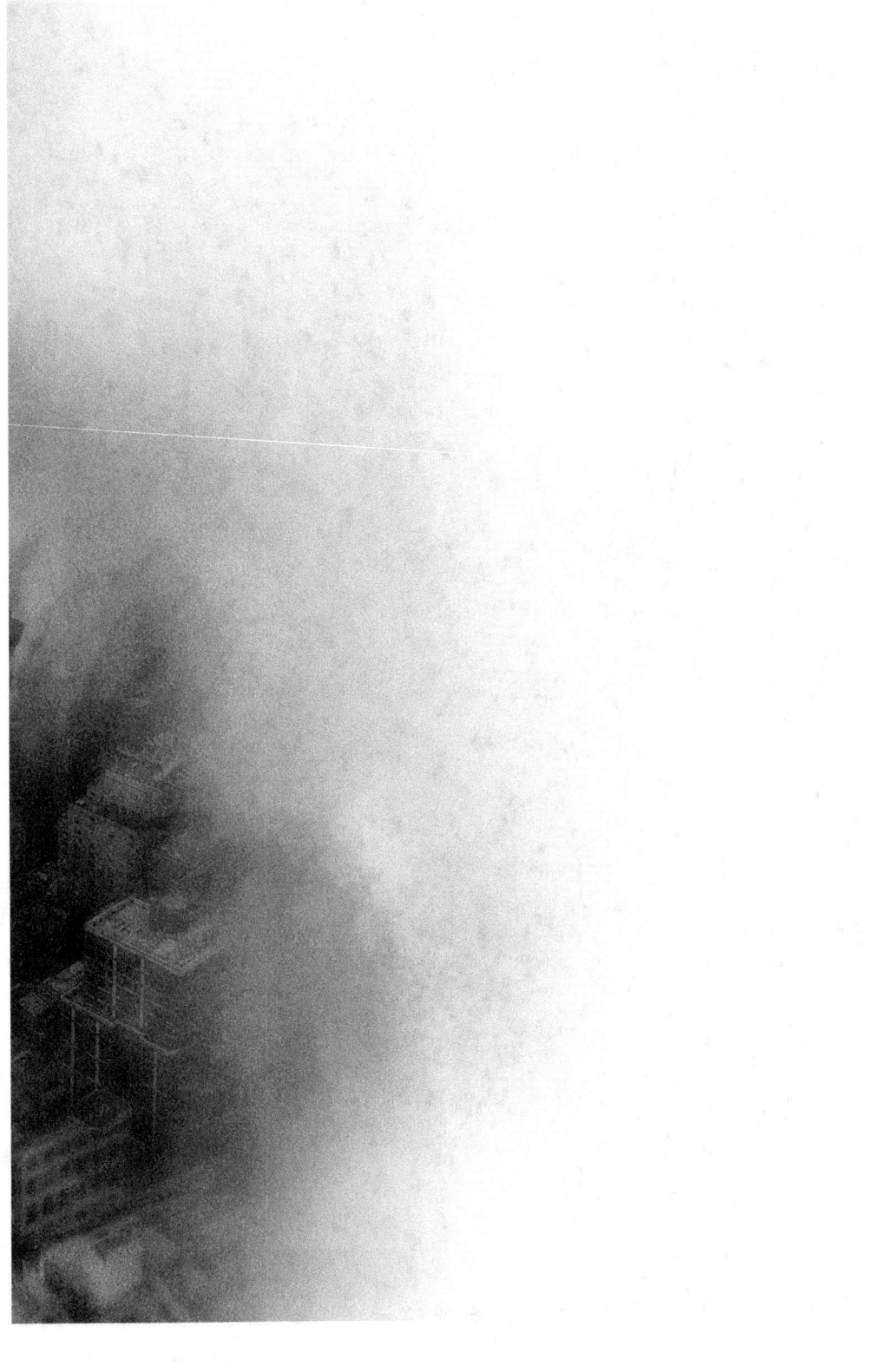

# CHAPTER
## FORTY—SEVEN

In the sprawling hangar bay, Maximus stood pensively. Although seasoned in combat, the recent conflict and its astonishing conclusion had left him grappling with the scale of what had unfolded. Around him, the air was thick with tension and disbelief.

Meanwhile, Ron lay trembling in the infirmary, the aftermath of his extraordinary actions visibly taking a toll on him.

"I can't believe he killed them," Eric muttered, his voice tinged with a mix of awe and horror.

"He didn't," Christopher interjected as he hurried over, his eyes wide with excitement rather than fear. "He didn't kill them; he did something... unbelievable."

The group turned their gaze towards Ron, their expressions a mix of reverence and confusion.

"You are something else," Lily whispered, her voice a soft echo in the vast hangar.

Eric's stare lingered on Ron, his face hard with unresolved emotions.

"Chris," Maximus intervened, his tone demanding clarity, "what did you mean he didn't kill them? How do you know?"

Christopher's laughter broke the heavy atmosphere. "Because I was analyzing the energy he released. It wasn't lethal; it wasn't plasma or any destructive force. He conjured a distortion field—a wormhole, if you can believe it. I don't know where he sent them, but they're not dead."

"How is that possible?" Elizabeth asked, her curiosity piqued.

"You tell me," Christopher quipped, the levity in his voice failing to mask the seriousness of their discovery.

Maximus addressed the group, his voice firm yet fatigued. "Everyone performed admirably today. I'm proud of you all. We need to rest now. Keep a close watch on Ron, and we'll reconvene in the morning."

As the team dispersed, Maximus turned to Christopher, needing more answers. They retreated to the control room where Christopher summoned a halo screen, beckoning Maximus closer as if to share a secret.

"I can say this for certain: we're being watched," Christopher revealed, his voice a blend of worry and wonder. "I merged with Tara and discovered embedded surveillance programs in our system—sub-routines designed to monitor our every move."

Maximus, familiar with Eagle Eye's methods, nodded. "I figured as much. Did you find the list?"

"With a bit of finesse and my brilliance, yes," Christopher boasted. "Tara and I retrieved it."

"And she has a name highlighted," Maximus noted, pointing at the screen.

They both read the name aloud: "Kaui Clark."

Maximus's gaze remained fixed on the screen. "What else did you find?"

Christopher switched the display to show a DNA strand. "I've analyzed everyone's DNA. All of us have the same anomaly, except for Ron. His is uniquely different. Given what happened today, I think I understand why."

He switched the screen to display another complex image.

"Is that what I think it is?" Maximus breathed, barely audible.

"It's exactly what you think. It resembles the nucleus of a star..."

Maximus absorbed the implications, a heavy sense of both wonder and concern settling over him.

Just what on Earth was Ron evolving into?

# CHAPTER
## FORTY—EIGHT

In the shadowy confines of her office, Eagle Eye stared intently at surveillance footage. Her secure phone suddenly rang, breaking the silence. "Everything went according to plan, and they have no idea we're inside the Parthenon," she reported confidently.

The voice on the other end was Zaccarie's. "Excellent, phase one is complete. They won't even see what's coming."

"What about Ron? He's definitely a problem."

"In the way?" Zaccarie's laughter was malicious and cold. "Oh my dear, he is not just a problem—he's our greatest asset." The line went dead, leaving Eagle Eye to ponder her increasingly complex life.

She had been a fighter from the start, raised in isolation by an agency that had honed her intellect and physical capabilities from a young age. Eagle Eye had never experienced the childhood privileges of love, compassion, or nurturing. Emotions had been alien concepts to her until she met Maximus Curton.

It was Eagle Eye who had recruited Maximus into the FBI. After his training, they had fought side by side for years, and their partnership had deepened into love. However, their relationship was short-lived. There was always a part of Eagle Eye that felt incomplete, a void she was desperate to fill, and secrets that gnawed at her conscience—secrets she could never share with Maximus, the man she loved.

She knew the truth about Maximus's father's death; it was a hit ordered by Aegeus Lorenz over a failed business deal that could have propelled the Lorenz Corporation to new heights.

One day, Eagle Eye had accidentally overheard a conversation that Le Meire was having. She couldn't identify the other speaker, but the topic was clear: Zaccarie must never learn of the child. Aegeus Lorenz had been determined to remove any obstacles to his son's ascent to power, regardless of the personal costs involved.

Armed with such explosive knowledge for many years, even Eagle Eye, as ruthless as she was, found herself questioning her boundaries. Where did her loyalty end, and her morality begin? Could she continue on this path, or was it time to rethink the choices that had defined her life?

# CHAPTER
## FORTY—NINE

**M**aximus approached Elizabeth's quarters and knocked on the door. He had grown quite fond of her; her grace and beauty had moved him in ways he hadn't felt for a long time, especially after witnessing her valor in battle. "Get a grip," he muttered to himself as he stood at her door, regretting the conversation he was about to have, yet knowing it was necessary.

"Come in," Elizabeth called from the other side.

"Hey," was all Maximus managed as he entered.

"Hey yourself," she replied with a smile.

"You were incredible today."

"Thanks, it's all thanks to your training," she said, her eyes reflecting admiration.

"That's actually why I'm here, Elizabeth. You might be wondering why I stopped training you prematurely."

The thought had crossed her mind, but she had assumed he had his reasons. "I did wonder," she admitted, noting that he hadn't used the nickname 'Lizzy,' which she had grown to like.

"I stopped because I can't train you anymore," he blurted out.

"I'm not following...."

"Elizabeth, I've taught you everything I know, and you've surpassed my training. There's literally nothing left for me to teach you."

Her heart sank a little. "So, what does this mean?"

"It means you need a new teacher; someone far more powerful and skilled than I."

"I don't think I like where this is going," she said hesitantly.

"You may not, but it's necessary. You need to complete your training and become who you're meant to be, and you can't do that confined here in the Parthenon."

Elizabeth sat down on her bed, overwhelmed by the weight of his words. She knew deep down she had to leave, that there was more for her to learn and experience.

"What about Madison? I can't just leave her..."

"Madison will be fine here with us. I will personally watch over her," Maximus reassured her, sitting beside her. "But you must complete your training for the battle that I fear is ahead."

She knew this was just the beginning. The thought of leaving her daughter was excruciating, but she also knew that Madison would be safe. They had always been just the two of them, surviving day by day, but this was about something much bigger than daily routines. This was about the future.

"What do I have to do?" she asked finally.

Maximus stood and pulled a scroll from beneath his shirt, handing it to her. "This scroll contains instructions on how to reach the master you seek. His name is Izza Ne. You must find him, and only then will he train you."

"How am I supposed to do that?" she asked, puzzled by the mysterious task.

"Only you can figure that out. It's part of your journey. I found him, so I have no doubt you will too."

"When do I leave?"

"Now," he replied, his voice tinged with sadness.

Maximus briefly placed his hand on her shoulder before turning to leave, his heart heavy. He had just sent the woman he cared for on a potentially perilous journey from which she might never return.

Elizabeth packed quickly, her heart torn between her duty and her love for her daughter. As she departed, she looked back at the Parthenon, wondering if Madison would understand her decision. She made a promise to herself: when she returned, she would be at the zenith of her power.

With determination, Elizabeth Duncan set out on her journey, leaving behind her old life and stepping into a destiny that awaited her.

# MAXIMUS "MAX" CURTON

MAXIMUS CORTON IS A CONFIDENT, LOYAL AND CHARISMATIC COLLEGE PROFESSOR WHO IS ADMIRED BY EVERY STUDENT ON CAMPUS. HOWEVER, HIS LIFE BEFORE ACADEMIA WAS LIVED IN THE DARKEST CORNERS OF THE MILITARY. HIS PAST IS FILLED WITH TERRIBLE CHOICES AND THE RUTHLESS DECISIONS MADE IN THE NAME OF WHAT WAS PERCEIVED AS "THE GREATER GOOD". MAXIMUS TRIED TO LEAVE THE BURDEN OF HIS PAST BEHIND AND COMMENCE A NORMAL LIFE IN WHICH HE COULD HELP PEOPLE AND BETTER THE WORLD SOMEHOW. HOWEVER, WHEN THE WAVE HITS, HE IS ONCE MORE THRUST INTO A WORLD WHERE LIFE AND DEATH HANG IN THE BALANCE OF EVERY MOVE HE MAKES. WITH HUMANITY AT A CROSSROADS WITH THE EMERGENCE OF THE SHIFTS, MAXIMUS VOWS TO USE ALL HIS KNOWLEDGE AND WISDOM TO ENSURE THAT HE CAN SET PEOPLE ON THE PATH TOWARDS PEACE, JUSTICE AND HARMONY.

# MAXIMUS "MAX" CURTON

MAXIMUS CORTON IS A CONFIDENT, LOYAL AND CHARISMATIC
COLLEGE PROFESSOR WHO IS ADMIRED BY EVERY STUDENT ON
CAMPUS. HOWEVER, HIS LIFE BEFORE ACADEMIA WAS LIVED IN
THE DARKEST CORNERS OF THE MILITARY. HIS PAST IS FILLED
WITH TERRIBLE CHOICES AND THE RUTHLESS DECISIONS MADE IN
THE NAME OF WHAT WAS PERCEIVED AS "THE GREATER GOOD".
MAXIMUS TRIED TO LEAVE THE BURDEN OF HIS PAST BEHIND AND
COMMENCE A NORMAL LIFE IN WHICH HE COULD HELP
PEOPLE AND BETTER THE WORLD SOMEHOW. HOWEVER, WHEN
THE WAVE HITS, HE IS ONCE MORE THRUST INTO A WORLD
WHERE LIFE AND DEATH HANG IN THE BALANCE OF EVERY MOVE
HE MAKES. WITH HUMANITY AT A CROSSROADS WITH THE
EMERGENCE OF THE SHIFTS, MAXIMUS VOWS TO USE ALL HIS
KNOWLEDGE AND WISDOM TO ENSURE THAT HE CAN SET PEOPLE
ON THE PATH TOWARDS PEACE, JUSTICE AND HARMONY.

# ZACCARIE LORENZ

ZACCARIE LORENZ IS A MANIPULATIVE NARCISSIST WITH AN
INSATIABLE NEED - AND ABILITY - TO USE
OTHERS AS HIS PLAYTHINGS. HE'S ARROGANT, CALM, PATIENT
AND INTIMIDATING BUT AT THE SAME TIME
IRRESISTIBLE AND CHARMING. HE IS A MAGNET WHO HOLDS THE
ATTENTION OF ANY ROOM HE IS IN.

IN HIS YOUTH, ZACCARIE WAS ON A PATH TOWARD BEING A
GOOD MAN. HE BELIEVED IN COMPASSION AND EVEN FELL IN
LOVE, BUT A SERIES OF TRAGIC EVENTS DARKENED HIS OUTLOOK,
AND THE AMBITIONS OF HIS LATE FATHER TWISTED HIS
MORALITY TOWARD PURE AMBITION. ANY TRACES OF ANYTHING
RESEMBLING LOVE ARE BURIED BENEATH HIS VISIONS
OF DOMINATION MAKING HIM THE OPPOSITE SIDE OF THE SAME
COIN AS MAXIMUS WHO WISHES TO BENEFIT ALL
IN HIS ENDEAVORS. WHEN THE WAVE GIVES HIM THE POWER TO
TRANSFORM MATTER, HE TAKES THIS ONLY AS THE
NEXT LOGICAL STEP IN HIS PLANS. ZACCARIE SEES HIMSELF
SITTING ATOP A GOLDEN THRONE WITH ALL OF HUMANITY
BOWING AT HIS FEET.